The Old Man
and the Bureaucrats

Other Phoenix Fiction titles from Chicago

MIRCEA ELIADE

The Old Man and the Bureaucrats

TRANSLATED BY
Mary Park Stevenson

THE UNIVERSITY OF CHICAGO PRESS
Chicago & London

The University of Chicago Press, Chicago 60637
The University of Chicago Press, Ltd., London

*Reprinted by arrangement with the University of
Notre Dame Press.*

Library of Congress Cataloging in Publication Data
Eliade, Mircea, 1907–
    The old man and the bureaucrats.
    (Phoenix fiction)
    Translation of: Pe strada mantuleasa.
    I. Title.   II. Series.
[PC839.E38P413   1988]   859'.334   88-4833
ISBN 0-226-20410-3 (pbk.)

I

FOR SEVERAL MINUTES THE OLD MAN WALKED BACK AND forth in front of the house, not daring to enter. It was a plain facade with many stories, almost severe, like a building constructed around the turn of the century. Along the sidewalk the chestnuts still cast a little shade, but the street was intensely hot. The sunlight struck it with the full strength of the summer noon, and the old man took out his handkerchief and wrapped it around his neck. He was rather tall and very thin, and he had a long face that was bony and drab, with gray expressionless eyes. His neglected mustache might have been white had it not been yellowed slightly by tobacco. He wore an old straw hat, and his faded summer suit was too large. It looked as if it did not belong to him.

He saw the officer approaching and greeted him from a distance, lifting his hat. "Can you tell me the time?" he asked with excessive politeness.

"Two," replied the officer, without looking at his watch.

"Thank you very much." The old man smiled and nodded several times, then stepped resolutely up to the entrance of the building. As he placed his hand on the latch he heard the officer behind him.

"You have to push the button first."

Startled, the old man turned his head.

"I live here, too," said the officer, reaching to carry out his instructions. A moment later he asked without turning around, "Whom do you want?"

"*Domnul** Borza, Major of the MAI."**

"I don't know if he's at home. At this time he's usually at the office." He spoke in a neutral voice, staring straight ahead.

The door opened and the officer let the old man enter. He continued to avoid looking at him and greeted the porter, who had appeared in the dimly lighted lobby.

"This gentleman is looking for the Comrade Major," said the officer, going toward the elevator.

"I don't know if he's at home," commented the porter. "It would be better to go to the police station."

"I have an appointment with him," the old man said. "I come on behalf of the family." He added pointedly, "You might say that for him—*domnul* Major—I *am* part of the family. I'm the most precious part—childhood. . . ."

The porter looked at him doubtfully, shaking his head. "You can try. He's on the fifth floor," he said at last, and went on quickly, "if he's at home. . . ."

The old man placed his hat under his arm and started toward the stairs.

"Wait a bit and you can take the elevator," the porter called after him.

Turning, the old man bowed respectfully. "Thank you very much. I can't abide the elevator. I prefer to climb the stairs. Especially when I go into a house the

*Mister, sir.
**Ministry of Internal Affairs (i.e., Police).

first time," he added, with a melancholy inflection, "I like to climb the stairs."

He went up steadily, without haste, holding the railing with his right hand and hugging his hat close under the other arm. When he found himself in front of the door to the apartment on the second floor, he stopped and leaned against the wall, fanning himself with his hat. He heard the voices of children, then the door opened suddenly and a woman of indefinite age came out quickly, an empty beer bottle in her hand. She was smiling, but when her eyes fell on the visitor her face became hard.

"Who do you want?"

"I was resting a moment," said the old man, bowing politely a number of times. "I'm on my way to the fifth floor to see *domnul* Borza, Major of the MAI. Do you know him?"

"Ask downstairs in the lobby," the woman responded curtly, twisting the beer bottle mechanically between her fingers. "The porter's there. He can tell you. . . ." She started to descend the stairs but reconsidered, turned back, and gave the bell several brief, nervous jabs. They heard the children's voices again, and a few minutes later the door opened and someone—the old man did not have time to see him—tried to put his head outside, but the woman pushed him back and disappeared at once behind the door. The old man smiled in embarrassment and, replacing his hat under his arm, started up the stairs again.

In front of the third floor apartment the officer was waiting for him. "You said you're looking for the Major," he whispered. "Why didn't you take the elevator?"

3

"I can't abide it," answered the old man, cowed. "Especially in summer, in the heat, it goes to my head. I can't stand it."

"But what were you doing on the second floor?" the officer inquired, still whispering. "Do you know anyone on the second floor?"

"No, I don't know anyone. I only stopped to catch my breath, and just then a lady came out and asked me . . ."

"What did she ask you?" interrupted the officer, leaning toward the old man.

"As a matter of fact she didn't ask me anything important—just whom I was looking for. And I answered . . ."

"I understand," the officer broke in abruptly. Then after glancing at the floor above, he moved closer to the visitor and inquired in a whisper, "Do you know the Major well?"

"I've known him since he was so high. . . ." The old man smiled and indicated with his hand a certain height from the floor. "I can say that I'm part of the family, perhaps even more than family. . . ."

"Aha!" exclaimed the officer, "That means you know him well. So that's how you found out his address! Because he's just moved here. I know him well, too," he added. "We've worked together. He's a solid citizen, very trustworthy."

They heard the sound of the elevator and the officer paused a moment in confusion; then without adding more, without a parting word, he opened the door of the apartment and went in. The old man leaned against the wall and commenced to fan himself again with his hat.

Smoothly and silently the elevator went by and as it passed he caught sight of a pale face with two large violet eyes gazing penetratingly at him. He waited a few moments longer, then decided to continue his climb. The elevator had stopped at the fourth floor and the youth whom he had seen was waiting there for him, holding the door open.

"Get in," he said. "I get off here."

"Thank you very much," said the old man. "I didn't take the elevator because I can't abide it. I prefer to climb on foot—slowly," he explained with a smile, "like in the mountains."

"It'll be hard. Three more floors." The youth's face was uncommonly pale.

"Fortunately," and the old man fanned himself with his hat, "I can say that I've arrived."

"Oh, have you come to see the Comrade Engineer?" asked the youth, surprised, pointing to the door before him. "I don't think you'll find him at home. Did you announce yourself downstairs to the porter?" He dropped his voice suddenly.

The old man shook his head several times and smiled in embarrassment. "I've expressed myself badly . . . I should have said, 'I'm nearly there.' I'm going to the fifth floor."

The young man blinked repeatedly and pulled out his handkerchief in haste. He began to wipe his hands nervously.

"The Comrade Major? If only he's in. Usually he lunches at the commissary. Do you know him well?" he asked, looking intently into the old man's eyes. "I haven't seen you here before. . . ."

"He's just moved," said the old man. "I knew him when he was so high. . . ."

Irresolute, the youth continued to twist the handkerchief between his fingers for a moment, then pressed the button of the elevator and sent it back downstairs.

"Do you know his family, too?" he asked in a whisper, glancing several times at the floor above.

"I can say that I'm part of the family . . ."

"Then you're from the country," interrupted the youth. "His family's from the country. I knew his brother in the *Parafina*. He's an exceptional character. An old fighter. I know him very well."

No doubt he would have continued, for he approached the old man with a mysterious smile, but he heard steps on the stairs and drew back rapidly toward the door. Turning his back, he began to search nervously for his key.

"I'm glad to have met you," said the old man, bowing, and he set out again with his hand on the railing. On the stairs he met a couple, whom he greeted. The woman's hair was cut short and she was dressed in some kind of uniform with a badge pinned to her blouse. The man, much younger than she, walked awkwardly and seemed to avoid looking at her, but after they passed they both stopped and turned their heads to see what the old man was doing. He had stopped before the door and taken out his handkerchief to wipe his face, then he smoothed the lapels of his coat with the back of his hand. He seemed to be about to ring when he thought better of it and started back toward the stairs with an unusually nimble step. Pausing a few steps from the couple, who were waiting in astonishment near the wall, he bowed politely.

"If it's not too much trouble could you tell me the time?" he asked the woman.

"Two," she replied, "five past."

"Thank you, and my apologies . . . I have an appointment around two."

He climbed the stairs again rapidly and rang the bell a long time. A young woman, wearing excessive makeup applied without skill, opened the door.

"*Sarut mainile, conita,*"* said the old man, bowing. "I hope I haven't come too early, nor too late. I said to myself, 'Two, two-five, is just the right time.'"

"He's at lunch," the woman told him, revealing several gold teeth when she smiled. "He was expecting you at a quarter after two, or two-thirty. . . ."

"Then I'll wait, I'll wait." He started to withdraw.

"No, come in. It's cooler in here. It's a bourgeois apartment," she added pleasantly.

"I know, I know," said the old man. "He's just moved."

"The other one on *calea*** Rahovei was too far from the office. And it wasn't appropriate for a Major of the MAI with such important assignments. It was too small. It didn't have a piano or a radio."

"I know, I know," repeated the old man, suddenly in a very good humor. "And him—I knew him when he was so high . . ." and he measured the height with his hand.

The woman began to laugh. "Please come into the salon," she said, taking him into a spacious room that was furnished conservatively but with elegance. "I'll tell him you've come."

---

*A polite greeting: I kiss your hands, ma'am.
**Street or way.

With a smile the old man sat down on the sofa and began to rub his knees happily with his hands. A few moments later, however, the woman reappeared and motioned him to get up.

"He says to come into the study, he'll be with you right away."

She led him into an adjacent room, indicating a large leather armchair in front of the bookcase. The old man thanked her, sat down, and commenced rubbing his knees again. Occasionally he leaned closer to the shelves to read the titles of the books. When he heard the door open he stood up excitedly. A robust man, swarthy, almost fat, stood in the doorway looking at him. He had black hair, purple cheeks, and thick eyebrows that almost touched. His little steely eyes were hidden behind blue lids that were swollen and splotched. He was in shirt and braces, with his sleeves rolled up, and when he entered the room he was laughing, a napkin still tucked into the front of his shirt, but as soon as he saw the old man he frowned.

"What are you doing here?" he asked in a harsh, rough voice. "Which way did you come in?"

"Don't you recognize me?" the old man asked, astonished, with a tentative smile. "I knew you when you were so high. . . ." He extended his hand to the proper height above the carpet.

"How did you get in?" asked the Major, seizing one end of the napkin and beginning to wipe his mouth and face. "How did the porter let you get by?"

The old man continued to smile and explained, "I told myself that at two or two-fifteen I'd be sure to find you at home."

"But who are you?"

"You mean to say you don't recognize me?" The old man shook his head sadly. "It's true that more than thirty years have passed since then, but I've remembered you. And when I learned that you'd moved here, I said to myself, 'Why not pay him a visit and see if he recognizes me?'"

"But who are you, *domnule*?" cried the Major with a threatening step in the old man's direction.

"On Mantuleasa Street . . ." the other began, shaking his head, "wasn't there a school on Mantuleasa Street with chestnut trees in the yard and a garden in back with apricot and cherry trees? It's not possible to forget this! It's here, just two steps away." He nodded toward the window. "I seem to see you now. You wore a sailor suit and you were sweating—you always did sweat a lot!"

The Major left the room abruptly, slamming the door behind him. "Aneta!" he called as he strode through the salon. "Aneta!"

Presently the woman appeared.

"Did you bring this character into the study?" he asked, lowering his voice. "Didn't I tell you not to receive anyone, to send them all to the Ministry? Didn't I tell you I'm expecting an Inspector at two-fifteen or two-thirty?"

"Why, I thought that's who this was, if the porter let him in. And I though he said something . . . that he knows you well, or that he himself was the Inspector."

The Major crossed the salon again with great strides and went back into the study. "Do you mean to tell me that you got in here fraudulently?" he asked, squinting at his uninvited guest, "you told my wife that you were the Inspector!"

9

"I didn't say that," protested the old man with dignity, "but I could have said it because I am an inspector. Retired, but it can be said that I'm still an inspector. . . ."

"But who are you, *domnule?*" the Major exclaimed again, snatching the napkin from his neck and twisting it in his hands, wringing it and snapping it as if it were a strap.

"You still don't remember? Mantuleasa Street? When you went to the primary school on Mantuleasa Street, and at recess you climbed the cherry trees, and once you hurt your head in a fall, and the Principal of the school took you in his arms and carried you to the teacher's room and dressed the wound? And the next day was the tenth of May celebration and you were very proud that you came with your head bandaged? And the Principal asked you, 'How's your head, *ma* Borza?' And you answered, 'I'm afraid of the poems, *domnule* Principal'—because you didn't like to memorize at all," the old man added, smiling. "'I'm afraid I won't be able to learn them by heart anymore. . . . ' *Ei bine,* the Principal—that's me. Teacher Farama, Zaharia Farama, fifteen years Principal of the Mantuleasa School and then school inspector, Class II, until I retired on a pension. . . . Don't you remember yet?"

The Major had been listening to him attentively, frowning. "You're making fun of me," he began, hissing the words through his teeth. "If you weren't an old man I'd arrest you on the spot. You got into my house by claiming to be an inspector . . ."

"I didn't say that."

"Don't interrupt when I'm talking to you!" commanded the Major, advancing in a threatening manner.

10

"You got into my house through fraud but you must have had some purpose. Now, tell me quickly before I get mad, why did you come? What's your game?"

The old man passed a trembling hand over his face and sighed involuntarily. He lowered his voice. "Please don't be angry. Perhaps I'm in error. If so, I apologize. But aren't you *domnul* Vasile I. Borza, Major of the MAI?"

"That I am. Not *domnul,* but Comrade Major Borza I. Vasile. What about him? How does he interest you?"

"Then, excuse me, but you went to my school on Mantuleasa Street. I can tell you the years—between 1912 and 1915. You see, even though more than thirty years have passed, I still remember. In each class I became attached to a few boys, not always prizewinners," he added with a smile, "but boys whom I felt to be something special. And then I followed them as well as I could through the *liceu** and the university. . . . It's true, I lost track of you, but the war came in 1916 and this explains a great deal. I heard that you'd left for the provinces. . . ."

The Major listened carefully, turning his head now and then toward the adjoining room.

"Listen, *domnule* Principal," he began, his tone less aggressive but still sharp. "I'm not what you think I am—with all that *liceu* education, and the university. I'm from the people. I've been persecuted in my lifetime and I haven't had the time or the money or the opportunities to get a fancy education."

"I was talking about the primary school on Mantuleasa."

"I told you not to interrupt when I'm speaking to

*A secondary school.

you," said the Major, looking directly into his eyes. "These questions of titles and secondary schools—we know the story. But those times have gone, with their privileges, diplomas, and cock and bull tales. We've buried your regime," he added, turning again to glance at the next room. "The regime of the exploiters," he cried, raising his voice suddenly. "Now the working people have their say! Get this into your head while there's still time. Understand?"

"I understand," said the old man, bowing his head. "Please forgive me. It was a mistake. It was unintentional. . . ."

After regarding him for a long time the Major smiled. "I hope it was a mistake, because otherwise you're in for it. And now, you can thank God that I'm not angry—and beat it!" He motioned quickly toward the door.

"My regards to you," said Farama. "My respectful regards. . . . Once more, please excuse me. . . ." Frightened, he backed out of the room and crossed the salon hastily.

Borza began to laugh, suddenly well-disposed. "Aneta!" he shouted from the door. "Quick! Bring the coffee!" He went to the other door and opened it.

"What do you say, Dumitrescu, about this nuisance?"

A rather young man came from the dining room. He had sleek chestnut hair and a tiny mustache above a small mouth with unusually thin lips. One almost had the impression that he had no lips at all. His pale eyelids covered eyes that had a somewhat yellow tinge in his gray and sickly face.

"Rather suspicious," he said with a strained smile. "It seems rather suspicious to me. . . ."

Borza's face changed. "That's the way it looks to me, too. He claimed that he confused me with someone else, but can you believe that?"

"The question of confusion of names is obviously false. I can't believe there are two Borza I. Vasile's of the same age in the same city. This fellow knows something," he added with a grin. "He's up to something. You notice that he knew your address, although you've just moved."

"I'll arrest him!" Borza exploded. "I'll arrest him right now!"

"Wait! Don't rush it," said Dumitrescu, going to the window. "If he's up to something we'd better follow him first." He pulled back the curtain and looked down at the street. "He's not down yet. . . . He seems very suspicious to me," he added, continuing to watch the street. "But actually, maybe the whole thing's more complicated. Maybe he's not confused about you, and that proves he's up to something, that he knows who you are. Maybe he's right. You might have gone to his school on Mantuleasa Street."

"Be serious, *domnule!*" Borza frowned. "Everybody knows I'm of the people, that I didn't go to school. . . ."

"Borza," said Dumitrescu, without turning around, "it isn't a disgrace if you went to the primary school on Mantuleasa Street. The poor and honest people were able to go to primary school too, under the past regime. . . ."

"But what if I tell you I didn't go to school on Mantuleasa Street?" exclaimed Borza. "I don't even know where it is."

"It's right here, nearby," said Dumitrescu, pressing his face to the glass.

"Could be, but I tell you—and I repeat it—I don't know it. I was raised in Tei. My father was a teamster. . . . But what's happened to that woman? Why doesn't she bring the coffee?" He whistled angrily through his teeth and started to leave the room. "The Inspector will be here any minute now and we wanted to drink our coffee in peace."

"He's come out on the street." Dumitrescu opened the window and leaned his head out. "You'll have to phone downstairs and have him followed. . . . Don't act rashly," he added, turning and staring at Borza. "This man knows something, he's up to something. Be careful. . . ."

II

AT DAWN THE NEXT DAY FARAMA WAS AWAKENED BY A
Security agent. "Come with me for questioning! Don't
take anything with you. You won't be staying long. . . ."

Several more agents were in the yard, while in front
of the house a car was waiting. They climbed into it in
silence, and suddenly Farama began to tremble.

"A summer day . . ." he said presently and tried to
smile.

The car stopped in front of the Security building. The
men led him through a number of long corridors and into
a vast, dirty elevator that was used for transporting materials to the top floor, still under construction. Farama
didn't notice how many times the elevator stopped before
the door on the opposite side opened and they set out
along a corridor that was dimly lit by a few globes hanging here and there from the ceiling. They went down
some steps and entered another hall which seemed to be
in a different building. It had large clean windows and a
gleaming new parquet floor. The walls had recently been
painted white. Before one of the numerous doors one of
the agents motioned to Farama to wait while he went in
alone. Presently he came back, accompanied by a round-
shouldered clerk with a stack of file folders under his
arm. Again they started out, still following the corridor
which seemed to describe a long semicircle. Stopping in
front of another elevator, they boarded it and went down.

Farama tried to count the floors but he found himself wedged between two agents, and since the clerk with the folders was in front of him, he could see nothing. When they got out they met a large group of people waiting to take their places in the elevator. From the corner of his eye Farama noticed that there were several uniformed Security agents scattered among the civilian clerks who were carrying files under their arms. This time they did not go far. The clerk with the folders stopped before the first door on the right and entered without knocking. A short time later a young man, whose eyeglasses gave him an intellectual air, beckoned to one of the agents to follow him. Soon after that the door opened and the clerk who had been carrying the folders appeared. Looking intently into Farama's eyes, he began to question him.

"You say you're Farama Zaharia, former Principal of Primary School No. 17 on Mantuleasa Street?"

"Yes," replied the old man solemnly. "I was also school inspector, Class II," he added, trying to clear his throat.

The clerk looked at him again with a slight frown and murmured to himself, "Strange. . . ."

Then he disappeared again and it was some time before he returned. Farama's knees had begun to ache and he stood first on one foot, then the other.

"Please come in," said the clerk, and they went into a room that resembled a reception room, with one window and several doors. A few benches lined the walls. The clerk approached the door next to the window and said without looking back, "Come with me."

In the office they entered there was a table with some telephones on it. Dumitrescu was waiting for them, leaning back in his chair and playing with his pencil.

16

"How long have you known Comrade Borza?"

"Since he was so high," said Farama, smiling and holding out his hand above the carpet. "I had him as a pupil in my school."

"How do you know it was he?"

Farama began to laugh, shaking his head sadly. "You see, this is where things are confused. Until yesterday at noon I could have sworn that it was he, *domnul* Major Vasile I. Borza. But I was at his house and he says he doesn't remember. . . ."

"But what did you want with Comrade Major Borza? How did you find out his address?"

"You see, it was like this," commenced Farama presently, preparing for a long tale. "Several weeks ago, in June, I was walking on the boulevard—because I still like to walk there near the school. I walk from the Pake Protopopescu statue on the boulevard and return by Mantuleasa. I was resting on a bench and I saw a truck stop in front of No. 138, right in front of me. Some young men got out, among them a number of militia, and they started to unload. Then someone came from the house and called to them to bring the things up. He cried, 'Comrade Major Vasile Borza is moving to the fifth floor.' Then I remembered him suddenly, when he was a little boy, Borza I. Vasile. And I remembered the incident of the rabbi's son. . . ."

"What incident?"

"Oh, that's a long story—long and strange. I could even say mysterious. The newspapers wrote something at the time but I don't think anyone figured it out. I'd say it's remained a mystery."

"What kind of incident? Why do you think it's still a mystery?"

"It's still a mystery because no one figured it out," replied Farama with sudden animation. "But in order to understand it you must know that Borza wasn't there from the start, in the cellar with the rabbi's son and Darvari and the others. Darvari Patru—this one I can tell you was right in the thick of things. This boy had a very inventive spirit. I followed him until late in his life, until he disappeared in his plane between the Island of the Serpents and Odessa. He vanished without a trace. This Darvari I'm telling you about discovered that a friend of his, Aldea, from the school on *calea* Mosilor, had been at Tekirghiol the year before and met a Tatar boy who earned his living by going from villa to villa exterminating flies. Yes, I'd say that's the right word—he exterminated them. If I hadn't seen it I wouldn't have believed it. Because I have to tell you that the following year I was in Tekirghiol and I met him too. This Tatar lad was extraordinary. I seem to see him now—a handsome, impetuous boy with his head shaved and eyes like two beads of steel. I seem to hear him—'Do you have many flies in the house?' He spoke perfect Romanian—he went to school in Constanta—but he spoke with a Tatar accent. 'Do you have flies in the house?' he would ask. First he'd knock at the door in order to attract attention, and then he'd ask from the hallway, without coming in, 'Do you have many flies?' He asked it like that in a tone that was a little bit ironic, as if he wanted to buy them, but just that way— for a song, a bargain. Let me tell you what happened to me. I'd heard about him but I hadn't seen him yet. I was expecting him. The villa where I'd found a room that summer was right on top of the hill. It was the last one in the town, 'Villa Cornelia,' it was called. That's why the

Tatar was late in coming to us, but he finally arrived, since this was his trade, the way he earned his living, exterminating flies. It was after lunch, two o'clock. I was asleep and when I heard him knock at the door—'Do you have flies?' he asks—I jumped up from the bed, I was that eager to meet him. I had flies like everyone in Tekirghiol, but what I was interested in was meeting him. 'I have plenty,' I replied. 'What will you do with them?' 'I'll banish them, and none will come for a week. If one does come back you don't give me any money.' 'How much?' 'One *leu*.* Half now and the other after a week. If you show me a single fly in your room I'll give back the half-*leu*.' 'Agreed,' I told him. 'Let's see what you can do!' And now, forgive me," Farama went on in a different tone, "but if you don't mind, I have a request to make."

"Speak up," encouraged Dumitrescu.

"I'd like to ask you to let me rest a moment on a chair. I'm about to collapse with fatigue. I suffer from a kind of rheumatism."

"Have a seat," said Dumitrescu, nodding toward a chair.

Farama bowed and sat down, breathing deeply. "Thank you very much. I saw from the first you have a good heart. You resemble a good friend of mine, Dorobantu."

"Never mind that," interrupted Dumitrescu. "I asked you what you wanted with Comrade Major Borza. You've rambled on a lot but you haven't answered me yet."

"You'll see. That's just what I was going to tell you about. I was there on the bench in front of No. 138 and I

*Romanian monetary unit equal to 100 bani.

remembered him when he was a pupil of mine at Mantuleasa, and I said to myself, I'll go see him. He's turned out well now. He's a Major. We'll have a talk, and recall when he was in school. I'll ask him if he knows anything more about Lixandru. Because in the fourth grade he made friends with Lixandru. They were like brothers. This Lixandru was a strange boy too, a dreamer, a kind of poet in his way, as a child of thirteen or fourteen. In fourth grade he was about that age because he had entered school late. He'd been sick for several years in a row, but when he came to me to school he was brilliant. He could have finished not just two, but three grades in a year—as he did, anyway, later in the *liceu*. . . . I wanted to ask the Major if he'd heard anything more about him."

"What did you say his name was?" asked Dumitrescu, starting as if he had just wakened.

"Lixandru. Gheorghita V. Lixandru."

"*Ei*, and what about him? What was his connection with Comrade Borza?"

"He had many" said Farama, nodding. "They were like brothers. When Lixandru ran away from home Borza hid him—not at his home, of course, but in a cellar in the *maidan*.* All these boys, I must say, had taken a great fancy to cellars and abandoned hovels after the incident I told you about, the one with the rabbi's son. At that time there was a *maidan* in front of the university called the Town Hall *Maidan*, and blocks of stone were piled on it for the new wing of the university which was built after the war. I seem to see them even now—large blocks of bluish-white stone . . ."

*Vacant lot.

20

"Never mind," Dumitrescu broke in. "You said something about a cellar and just now you said something more about a mystery and the rabbi's son. How is one related to the other?"

"They're related because the son of the rabbi disappeared in a cellar. He disappeared as if he'd never been on the face of the earth—without a trace, as if the earth had swallowed him. But I must be precise—what's true is true—he, this boy Iozi, knew that he would disappear and he told them goodbye. He hugged them all, then he dove into the water and no one saw him again."

"What are you talking about, *domnule?* Where did this happen?"

"In an abandoned cellar near the Church of the *Tei.*** But in order to understand you need to know all the story and it's a long tale. . . . May I light a cigarette?" he asked, humbly.

"Please do."

"Thank you very much." Farama took his pouch from his pocket. "I've been a great smoker in my life, but now I can say that I've given it up except for an occasional cigarette. I'll just roll one for myself," he added. "I don't suppose you smoke?"

"No."

"You're very wise," said Farama, busy with the cigarette. "I've heard that tobacco is a cause of cancer. . . ." He moistened the edge of the paper and put the cigarette in his mouth. Lighting it, he drew the first puff avidly, smiled and lowered his eyelids slightly, musing.

"It's a long story," he began. "For you to understand

**Linden tree.

21

it, you'll have to know that it all began with Abdul, the Tatar youngster of whom I spoke just now. As I told you, I too saw this fellow at work. He entered the room, sat down on the floor cross-legged, took out of his blouse a kind of leather purse and began to murmur unintelligible words in his language, Tatar. And then I saw what I've never seen in my life. I saw the flies gather like a black swarm above his head, and when they were all squeezed together like a ball, they rushed into the purse and Abdul closed it, putting it back in his blouse. He smiled and stood up. I gave him the half-*leu*, and I must add that for a whole week—but exactly a week—I didn't see a single fly in my room. They buzzed in the hall, a few still came up to the window, but to come in? Not one! After a week Abdul came to get the other half-*leu*. The next day, that is, on the eighth day after he made his spell, the flies invaded the room again and seemed to be even more numerous than before. Of course I called for him to come and get them. Three times he came during the three weeks that I stayed at the Villa Cornelia. . . . This is what I saw. But Aldea had already made friends with Abdul the year before. I don't know what he told him or how much he told him, but later I found out from Lixandru that Aldea had come back to Bucuresti in the fall with a secret that he'd learned from Abdul. From what I understood, the secret was something like this—that if they should sometime find an abandoned cellar full of water, they were to look for I know not what kind of signs, and if they found all the signs they'd know that the cellar was an enchanted place, that on that spot you could enter the nether world."

"Come now, *domnule!*" exclaimed Dumitrescu with a smile.

"Yes. It seems that Abdul taught him this. Perhaps he taught him other things, too, but Lixandru didn't tell me any more—it was Lixandru who told me all these things later. Aldea, Lixandru, and Iozi, the rabbi's son from *calea* Mosilor, began that year to go all over the *maidane* and all around the outskirts of Bucuresti to hunt for abandoned cellars. They found a lot of them but only two that were full of water, and, so Lixandru said, at only one were there signs that matched what Aldea had learned from Abdul.

"What kind of signs?"

"This I don't know because they didn't tell me—perhaps certain measurements. I found out later that the boys carried a long pole and an old pouch around with them. The pole was found broken in two but there was no trace of the pouch. Maybe the rabbi's son took it with him. What I know—because I learned all this at the investigation, and the newspapers wrote about it, too—what I know is that Lixandru dove into the water head first and stayed there for several minutes. But when he came out his face was white and he was shaking from the cold, and he told them, 'If I'd stayed a little longer you wouldn't have seen me anymore.' Then he added, 'But you know, it's just beautiful! It's like in a fairy tale.' Then Darvari dove in too, keeping his head down, but he came out immediately, his teeth chattering. 'I'll go down again tomorrow, because it's late now,' he said. Then two more boys jumped in, Aldea and Ionescu. The first knew how to swim underwater and stayed in a long time. The other, Ionescu, came out quickly, almost frozen. Aldea, though, who was a good swimmer, came to the surface several times and cried, 'I can't find it anymore! I found it a moment ago and now I've lost it. It's hidden again! It was

23

like the most brilliant light. . . . ' He dove once more to the bottom, stayed for some time and then came out, discouraged. 'It was like a diamond cave,' he told them, 'and it seemed to be lighted by a thousand flaming torches. . . . ' 'That's it!' cried the rabbi's son then. 'I know it, too!' And after he'd said goodbye to everyone and hugged Aldea and Lixandru he dove into the water head first and didn't come out again. The boys waited until evening, then they all went home, after swearing not to disclose the signs they knew to anyone. The next day Lixandru went to the rabbi to see if his son had returned, but he hadn't come back, and the police were searching all around the neighborhood. When the third day passed and the boy still hadn't returned Lixandru came to tell me about the incident. Borza was with him, although he hadn't been there when it happened.

"Then they began the investigations, but difficulties arose from the start, for the boys all said the water was deep—more than two meters—since they didn't touch bottom easily. And yet when the police came there was scarcely one meter. They searched everywhere in vain, and finally brought a pump and took all the water out of the cellar, but it was no use. Later, when the investigation was resumed, they made excavations in the bottom of the cellar and came upon an old wall, and the archaeological commission intervened and extended the area of excavation. They found the remains of medieval fortifications then, and deeper down, traces of human settlements even older; but of the rabbi's son—nothing."

"When did this happen?"

"In October 1915 at the beginning of the month, on the fourth or fifth."

Dumitrescu made a note of the date in a notebook. "In what part of the city is this cellar located?"

"It was near Obor on the *maidan* that stretched at that time between Obor and the beginning of Boulevard Pake Protopopescu. I saw it, too, as well as the excavations of the archaeological commission, but there's nothing left now. After the Germans came in November 1916 they made a munitions depot there and blew it up when they withdrew. Nothing remained of all the diggings. After the war the whole area was built up and now it's covered with new houses."

"And Borza was with you?"

"He came with Lixandru. He knew about it but he hadn't been with them at the time."

"Good." Dumitrescu smiled. "Enough for today. We'll talk again." With a preoccupied air he pressed a button. "Take *domnul* Principal to Room B," he said to the officer who entered. "Serve him dinner from the cafeteria."

"Thank you very much," said Farama, rising from his chair and bowing several times.

III

ON THE FOURTH DAY DUMITRESCU LUNCHED AGAIN WITH
Borza. When the coffee was served he said casually, playing with the toothpick and regarding vaguely some
wooden platters and peasant plates from Ardeal that were
hanging on the wall in front of him, "The people in Sec-
tion III went to the Academy Library and searched
through the collection of papers from 1915. You know,
Farama was right. Everything happened just as he told
us. Iozi, the son of the rabbi, dove into the water and
didn't come out again, and his body was never found. He
disappeared without a trace. . . . You never heard this
story? Don't you remember anything?" He turned his
head and looked into the other man's eyes.

"I've no idea who you're talking about," said Borza,
pulling out his napkin and wiping his face.

"I'm talking about your Principal, Farama, the man
from the Mantuleasa School."

Silently Borza laid the napkin on the table and leaned
back in his chair.

"Yes," Dumitrescu smiled and continued, "he's with
us. I'm holding him for questioning. He seemed suspect
to me. . . ."

"You mean . . ." began Borza, blushing. "You mean
. . . ? And that's why you changed the porter?"

"There's no connection. He's been given another assignment. But to return to your Principal, Farama, I can tell you he's a strange man with an extraordinary memory. He remembers the smallest details. He told me about you in the fourth grade, primary. . . ."

"But I told you, *domnule!* I don't know him. I didn't go to his school. I told you, I'm from Tei. I spent my childhood there—in Tei!"

"*Ei,* that's just the trouble, and I can tell you now because you brought up the subject. In your time there were only three primary schools in Tei—two for boys and one mixed."

"*Ei,* and what's that got to do with it?" interposed Borza nervously.

"It has to do because your name wasn't on the roll in any of these schools. . . ."

"How do you know that?"

"Because inquiries were made. . . ."

Suddenly Borza went pale, stared at him, then struck the table with his fist. "Aneta!" he shouted. "Quick! Bring some coffee and a bottle of rum!"

"I told you the Principal seemed suspect to me," continued Dumitrescu, unruffled. "And then we made inquiries. . . ."

"Wherever he is, that damned Principal, I'll roast him alive!" Borza struck his fist on the table again. "Give him to me for just one night and I'll take the rolls out of his hide! I'll teach him to be more careful with his denunciations and intrigues!"

With a grudging smile Dumitrescu shrugged his shoulders. "Comrade Borza," he began in a neutral voice, "it's no use getting angry with the Principal, because in this matter at least it's not his fault. That he's suspect is another story, and when we discover what he was after when he came to see you we'll tell you and you'll be happy. . . . But in the matter of you and the Mantuleasa School it's not his fault. Your name is found on the rolls there between the years 1913 and 1916, and not at any school in Tei. And since you've declared that you went to primary school—because without primary school you couldn't have been appointed directly to be major, first class—you don't have any reason to contradict Farama. So it's very probable that you went to Mantuleasa School and you've forgotten it. More than thirty years have passed since then. Who remembers what happened thirty years ago?"

"You suggest that I've forgotten . . ." Borza remarked thoughtfully. "You know, you may be right—I *have* forgotten. I had a difficult childhood. We were of the people. We were persecuted by society. . . ."

"But the things that happened to you, *domnule*, were terrific!" exclaimed Dumitrescu with admiration in his voice. "What friends you had! What curious characters! Like something from a novel."

"*Ei*, children!" said Borza with an embarrassed smile.

"No, it's something else," continued Dumitrescu with a trace of sadness in his voice. "You've known different times. You were a child before the other war, and you had the good luck to be friends with intelligent and enterprising boys. Especially that one, Lixandru, he called him, the one who shot with the bow . . ."

"I seem to recall something," Borza admitted, musing. "But to tell the truth," he added, "what's more interesting—I've forgotten. Now that you tell me about it I seem to remember someone who shot with a bow, but that's all."

Aneta entered with the tray of coffee and the bottle of rum. She set them on the table and started to sit down herself, but Borza signalled to her with his eyes and smiling in confusion she uncorked the bottle of rum, filled the two glasses and withdrew. After gulping his drink Borza seized the bottle and filled his glass again immediately.

"And now what do you intend to do?" he asked. "Will you hold him longer?"

Dumitrescu hesitated for some time, his fingers playing absently with the toothpick. "It doesn't depend on us," he observed. "First he'll have to finish writing his declaration. According to what he writes we'll investigate, and finally we'll find out what he wanted from you. Because one thing is certain—he's a suspicious character. All these stories about Mantuleasa School he's telling to gain time. No matter," he added, smiling, "we'll let him talk. We have time. We're not in a hurry."

"I wonder what he wanted from me," Borza remarked, speculating. "When you asked him what did he tell you?"

"*Ei,* I think it's here he made the first mistake," began Dumitrescu, becoming suddenly spirited. "He didn't realize that he made it, but when I listened to the recording the second time I was convinced that something had slipped out, that he'd betrayed himself involuntarily and had given us an important clue. He said he'd come to see you so the two of you could talk and reminisce about your childhood, and he'd ask you *if you knew anything more about Lixandru. Ei,* I don't know if you understand . . ."

"Seems like I understand something. . . ."

"You see? This Lixandru, according to Farama, was

29

closely associated with you and another boy, Darvari. And Darvari—I checked this out—vanished with his plane in 1930 between the Island of the Serpents and Odessa, and he was lost without a trace. Still, there are indications that he might have fled to Russia—and this—I don't know if you understand—in 1930. Now we're making inquiries. . . . But it's very probable that Farama met him again, perhaps even several times, many years after he'd finished military school, or after he'd received his pilot's license. Because Farama admitted that he often met Darvari's best friend, Lixandru. . . . Here's where I think we ought to look for the clue." Dumitrescu winked mysteriously.

"I don't remember it at all!" said Borza with an air of despair.

"And later when he told me how you all practiced archery, I was convinced that this was why he came to see you—to pump you about Lixandru and Darvari, to see if you'd found out anything more. Because I think you'll remember this—you all met on the Town Hall *Maidan* and shot with bows and arrows."

"Yes. We shot," nodded Borza.

"*Ei, bine!* Doesn't it seem strange to you that what happened, happened only to him, to Lixandru?" asked Dumitrescu, looking into Borza's eyes.

Borza gulped, then seized the glass of rum and drained it. "God strike me dead if I remember anything!" he exclaimed and started to wipe his face with his napkin.

"Then you have amnesia." Dumitrescu smiled. "You've lost your memory. . . ."

"You must be right. I've lost my memory because of

the beatings. I told you how I was tortured in the prisons of the *Prefectura** . . ."

" . . . because a thing like this, even after thirty years and more, can't be forgotten. You gathered on the *maidan* and shot with bows and arrows. You shot, of course, into the air, because you were scared when you didn't find Lixandru's arrow. This set you to thinking from the first. . . . Most of your shots were twelve to fifteen meters, but when Lixandru shot you saw the arrow flying above the stone blocks—those, you remember, that were piled on the *maidan* for the new university building—you saw it flying over the blocks, over the *maidan,* going toward the Bratianu statue. You took after it, frightened, because you thought some pedestrian would get hit. You searched on the boulevard around the statue, but you never found it, and after that you shot in the air. Each of you shot according to his strength, twelve, fifteen, a maximum of twenty meters. *Ei bine,* when Lixandru's turn came you saw the arrow fly up, up. You followed it with your eyes as long as possible until you all had stiff necks, then you didn't see it anymore and you sat down near the rocks, waiting for it to fall back. You were afraid because you thought it would fall with great force, and you stayed by the rocks so you could duck out of the way, but you waited like that for about two hours and the arrow never fell."

"You don't say!" exclaimed Borza, incredulous. "When did this happen?"

"According to Farama, in the spring of 1916, probably in April or May during Easter vacation. *Ei,* what do

*County or county council prisons.

31

you say?" Dumitrescu inquired with a knowing smile. "Doesn't it seem suspicious to you? Don't you see the connection? This is why he came to see you." Dumitrescu lowered his voice abruptly.

"Damn it!" Borza was overwhelmed. "You're right, of course. . . ."

Dumitrescu began to laugh amiably and filled his glass again with rum. "You don't have to get mad," he said. "We'll figure it out. We have to have a little patience. I told him to write all he knows about Lixandru and Darvari. Up to now he's asked twice for paper, twice in three days. His handwriting's beautiful, flowing, artistic, but he has a script that's hard to read. What he wrote until yesterday is being typed now, but as usual he digressed. I read all morning and still I haven't come to Darvari. He wrote a long tale about a friend of yours, a girl from Obor, Oana. Perhaps you recall her—Oana, daughter of a tavern-keeper. A terrific woman, this one. She was seven foot, ten. Farama began at the end—how, later, after Oana was married to her Estonian, they both willed their skeletons to the University of Dorpat. I requested inquiries to be made at Dorpat to see what's true in all this tale. I'm waiting now for the result."

IV

ALL THAT WEEK AND THE WEEK THAT FOLLOWED FARAMA spent leaning over the wooden table writing. On the second night he had been given another room in the old wing of the building, a little room with a chair and table and an iron bed minus its mattress. There was one window but he saw only the gray wall beyond it. Twice daily a guard came and brought him his meals from the cafeteria, giving him a receipt to sign. When Farama used up all the paper he would rise from the table and knock on the door. The guard would take the pile of written pages and return soon after with another bundle of sheets. Farama wrote on both sides, since he had been instructed to do so after finishing the supply of paper he had been given on the first day.

Whenever he was summoned to the interrogation they called his attention to his script and told him to write more legibly, so he tried to be careful and make each letter distinct and separate, but soon he permitted himself to be captured again by memories and he resumed his customary method of writing, which was difficult to decipher.

Farama suspected that the illegibility of his handwriting was the reason for his being called so often to be questioned. Sometimes he was asked at night to tell about what he had written during the day. The guard came to get him and they set out together, apparently never by the same route, for they were constantly traversing different corridors, descending and climbing various stairs, crossing large rooms which were either dark or else too brightly lighted, in which he saw here and there a militiaman struggling with sleep on a bench. Unexpectedly the guard would pause in front of a wall and press a button. An elevator would come to a stop behind them and they would descend or climb to another floor, where the guard would knock at a door and usher him into a well-lighted office. Behind the desk, playing with the pencil, Dumitrescu would be smiling and waiting for him.

This went on for two weeks. Then one day the guard opened the door and called to him from the threshold. "Please come with me."

Farama was writing and he turned his head, bewildered. "I've just begun," he began in a humble tone. "I've a terrific urge to write. . . ."

"Orders," explained the guard.

Farama laid the pen properly on the blotter, put the stopper in the bottle of ink, and went out. This time they did not go far. At the end of the hall the guard turned him over to a militiaman who was waiting for him and who took him to a different elevator. They went down into the courtyard, walked a few steps on the sidewalk along the wall, and entered another wing of the building. On the second floor the guard stopped and knocked at a door that was opened by a young man with a beaming countenance. He smiled all the time as he questioned the old man, "Are you Farama, Principal of the Mantuleasa School?"

"I am." Farama bowed politely.

"Come with me," continued the youth, and he added to the militiaman, "Wait downstairs."

They crossed a large room and the youth opened a door, motioning to Farama to go in alone. The office was spacious and luxuriously furnished, graced with many windows. At the desk sat a man of about fifty, gray at the temples, with a flat nose and very thin lips.

"*Ei!*" he greeted the old man jovially. "Tell me, Farama, what's this about Oana?"

"It's a long story," began Farama, embarrassed. "In order to understand it well you must first know the adventure of her grandfather, the forester. In my opinion it all started there, because her grandfather—who, when I knew him in 1915, was about ninety-six years old—had broken his agreement with the elder son of the Pasha of Silistra. This forester was taken when a child by the Turks when he tried to blow up the munitions dump of the garrison at Silistra. He was sentenced to be tied in a sack with rocks at his feet and thrown into the Danube. That's what the Turks did with the children of unbelievers. They didn't hang them or behead them, they drowned them. And the elder son of the Pasha saved this child. He begged them to give the boy to him as a slave, but they were close to the same age and became friends at once and were like brothers. They remained together about ten years. This Pasha's son was called Selim, and he would have been a great man in his country if the forester hadn't broken his agreement. But in order to understand how things happened, I must tell you that Selim's father, the Pasha, married him off when he reached the age of sixteen. He married him to two wives at once—a Turkish-Greek woman from Fanar, and a Turkish woman . . ."

35

"No, Farama," the man at the desk interrupted. "Not this. I asked you a precise question—what about Oana?"

"It will be hard to tell you," protested Farama, "because in my opinion it all started with the forester . . ."

"Forget the forester," the officer interrupted again, smiling. "Tell me what you know about Oana. When did you meet her? What was she like?"

Farama shook his head in despair. He seemed to be wondering how it would be possible to make himself understood unless he was permitted to relate it as it happened.

"When I met her," he began suddenly, "in 1915, she was thirteen and more than six feet tall. But she wasn't only tall, she was robust, broad-shouldered, and beautiful as a statue. Her eyes were black and she had long blond hair falling down her back, and she went around barefoot and jumped directly on a horse's back without a saddle, like a cossack woman—and she'd only ride skittish horses. When she was still a child the horse-traders took her with them to the fairs to mount their horses. That's what she was like when I met her. I remember even now. One of the parents came to me—a merchant from Armeneasca Street—to complain that his son was in bed because of a fight with the boys. 'Where was the fight?' I asked. 'He didn't want to tell me,' the merchant answered. 'Let me come with you and I'll find out,' I told him, and I took my hat and went with him to Armeneasca Street. I entered the boy's room alone. He was lying in bed, very pale. 'With whom did you fight, *puisor?*'* I asked. 'With Oana,' he said. 'With Uncle

*Sonny.

36

Fanica's Oana, of Obor. But we weren't fighting, we were just wrestling, because I'm the best at wrestling and the boys made me challenge her. She didn't want to wrestle with me but she lifted me by the back and whirled me around, although it was really just for fun—until one of the boys yelled, "Look, she hasn't any underpants on!" And then Oana threw me head over heels, and I fell, and later on the boys brought me home.' 'Good,' I told him. 'It's nothing. It will go away.' And when I saw his father, who was waiting for me in the hall, I said, 'Keep him home for a few days and I'll justify his absence; but it wouldn't be a bad idea for him to see a doctor.' And later I went to Obor. . . . And now forgive me, but if it's not too much trouble, I have a request to make," Farama added in a different tone.

"Say it."

"If I could just have permission to rest a moment in a chair. I suffer from a kind of rheumatism."

"Help yourself," consented the man behind the desk.

"Thank you very much," said Farama, sitting down on the chair to the left of the desk and beginning to rub his knees with the palms of his hands. "Yes," he resumed after a few moments, "I went to Obor that very afternoon. I found the tavern of Fanica Tunsu quickly, since it was well-known throughout the district. First I went into the tavern and asked for Tunsu. The innkeeper seemed to be an honest man, red-cheeked and healthy, but otherwise quite ordinary. 'You have a daughter, Oana,' I began. 'She's quite a sensation.' 'Her mother and I did what we could,' the innkeeper answered. 'The rest is from God. . . .' At the time I didn't understand very well what he meant, but when I went out into the yard it was made clear to me. I can say in truth that the rest was from God, who had blessed her beyond measure. Oana was wrestling with a farmhand, a country boy as big as a mountain. He had taken off his high boots and was only wearing his trousers. He strained with all his strength, but you could see that he was having trouble breathing. Oana had caught him around the ribs and was squeezing him enough to smother him; and then all at once she whirled him around a few times and threw him down in the dust, sitting on top of him in order to pin his shoulders to the ground. And I saw, too, that the boy had been right. At that time women still wore a kind of long bloomer, but Oana had nothing on underneath. She was like a statue, if you understand what I mean."

"And you say she was beautiful?" queried the other, thoughtfully.

"She was like a statue," repeated Farama, nodding, "because a statue you know, if it's well made, doesn't annoy you no matter how large it is. Oana was like that. If she'd simply gone about naked, it might not even have been noticed that she was especially big and strong, but when you saw her clothed she rather frightened you. She seemed like the daughter of a giant. And that's how the tale of Oana began, with a wrestling match. It's a long story. . . ." He paused and inquired, "May I smoke?"

"Certainly," the other replied in a distant voice, as if he had just been aroused from a reverie.

"Thank you very much." Farama selected a cigarette from the package and lit it. "But where to begin?" he wondered, after he had inhaled deeply the first puff. "I told you it's a long story, covering many years up to 1930; and if it had been up to me I'd have started it in 1840. It's a story that covers almost a hundred years. But let's say you know the beginning and we're now in 1915, the year I met her. The boys had already met and made friends with her several months before while they were roaming around the outskirts of the city in search of abandoned cellars, and among them all Oana was most friendly with Lixandru and Darvari. But the following summer, in 1916, the boys came to Obor every Saturday and Oana took them in the cart to see her grandfather in the forest of Paserea, where they'd stay until Monday morning. Oana liked them because they were all clever boys and not lacking in imagination. She had imagination enough too, although as you'll see, it was her own special kind. Many things happened there, those nights in the forest of Paserea. I never learned about all of them, but what I did find out was enough for me to understand why these boys embarked on such unusual courses. Because you should know that besides Lixandru, who was at that time about fourteen, the other five were children between the ages of eleven and twelve. I learned about the first incident from Ionescu. It seems that one night that summer around the beginning of June, Ionescu woke up because he was thirsty and he went out to look for the pail of water. The boys slept in a kind of grain loft near the house of the forester, right in the heart of the wood; and Ionescu, after he had had a drink, looked through the trees and thought he saw a ghost. He was afraid, but he soon realized that it was Oana and ran after her in his bare feet, because this Ionescu was by nature a curious child. The moon was shining and he could see her far ahead of him, but he only went a short distance, because Oana stopped at the edge of a clearing and took off her

39

dress and stood there naked. She knelt down first and searched for something among the weeds, then she stood up and began to dance around in a circle, singing and murmuring to herself. The boy didn't hear everything, but the refrain was clear: 'Belladonna, my good lady, marry me off within a month!' Ionescu, a child, didn't realize that it was a love-charm, a spell for marriage. He stayed there hidden behind a bush just a few meters away and prepared to scare her, but suddenly he saw her stop her dance, put her hands on her hips and cry, 'Marry me, *fa*! My brains are on fire!' And the next moment the boy stiffened as an apparition rose abruptly out of the weeds. It looked like an old woman clothed in tatters, her hair in disorder, a gold necklace at her throat. She hurried menacingly to Oana. 'Ha! Crazy fool!' cried the old woman. 'Ha! You're not even fourteen!' Oana fell on her knees and bowed her head. 'Calm down,' continued the old woman, 'because what's destined for you I can't undo. When the time comes for you to marry go to the mountains, because that's where your husband will come from—marvelous, like you, astride two horses, with a red kerchief at his throat. . . . ' And then, Ionescu said, the apparition was lost among the weeds, but this was enough for Oana, and from that time on she thought of nothing but the mountains. She didn't get to go that fall because the war came to Romania, too, yet she started out, but not alone. She took the boys with her. . . ."

"But how could her father permit her to leave like that, when she was only fourteen, and go alone with the boys to the mountains?"

"Ah," smiled Farama, "this is a long story. I wrote out part of it the day before yesterday. I don't know if you've had the opportunity to look over what I wrote. Her father let her go because that year the *Doftor* came again to see the forester, and this *Doftor* was endowed with strange powers."

"The Doctor? Doctor who? What was his name?"

"Only the forester knew what his real name was because he had known him as a child. People called him the *Doftor* because of his skill with all kinds of cures, and because he was always traveling in foreign lands, far away. He knew many languages, countless sciences, and he cured people and cattle with simple old wives' remedies, but his great weakness was performing feats of magic. He was unsurpassed at sleight-of-hand and he was also an illusionist, a fakir, and God knows what else, for he did incredible things. All this he did for his own pleasure and only at country fairs and small market towns, never at Bucuresti. This is what he loved best to do—take several children with him in two carts with six horses, and wander for a month or two through the villages between *Sfint** Petru and *Sfinta* Maria. That year he took with him Oana, Lixandru, Aldea, and Ionescu. They set out for Campulung and from there they headed for the mountains, but they couldn't go up the mountain because in the meantime Romania entered the war. . . . A great conjuror!" Farama exclaimed, shaking his head.

"Did you go to see him?"

"I saw him several times—at work, I mean, at his conjuring. The first time was at the forester's, in his yard—and I just couldn't believe it! It was on a Sunday toward evening and we were waiting for the horses to be

*Saint.

41

harnessed to the carriage so we could go home. There were about ten of us and we all had business in Bucuresti the next day. 'Stay a little longer and I'll show you something!' cried the *Doftor*, clapping his hands for silence. Then he began to walk back and forth in front of us with his hands in his pockets, frowning, thoughtful. Suddenly he lifted one hand and grasped something from the air. We looked at it closely and saw that it was a kind of thin thread of glass. He laid it on the ground and began to pull it and stretch it, and the thread soon became a pane about a meter and a half square, which he made fast in the ground, then seized one side and again began to pull and stretch it out behind him. In about two or three minutes he had made a glass reservoir several meters in size, a kind of enormous aquarium. Then we saw the water gush up powerfully from the earth and fill the tank to the brim. The *Doftor* made a few more motions and we saw many kinds of fish, large and brightly colored, swimming in the water. We were astounded. The *Doftor* lit a cigarette and turned to us, saying, 'Come closer. Examine the fish and tell me which one you want me to get for you.' We approached and indicated a large fish with a blue crest and red eyes. 'Ha!' said the *Doftor*. 'You've chosen well. This is *Ichthys Columbarius*, a rare fish from the South Seas.' And without removing the cigarette from his mouth he walked right through the glass like a shadow, and into the tank. He stayed there in the middle of it, in the water among the fish, for some time, where we could all see him perfectly. He walked around with the cigarette still burning between his lips, then he stretched out his hand and seized the *Columbarius*. He came out of the tank just as he'd entered it, passing through the glass with the cigarette in the corner of his mouth, and in his hands he held the fish, which he showed to us. We watched it struggle, but we were more interested in the *Doftor*. He didn't have a drop of water on him—not on his face nor on his clothes. One of the men took the fish in his hand, but it escaped immediately into the grass and we all leaped to catch it. The *Doftor* laughed. He captured the fish, put his hand through the glass of the tank and let the creature go free in the water. Then he clapped his hands, and the aquarium with the fish and all disappeared. . . ."

"Great illusionist!" exclaimed the man at the desk.

"The greatest! But this—what I'm telling you now—was nothing compared with what he used to do at the markets and fairs, especially that summer when he took Oana and the boys with him. You can imagine that after I'd seen him at Paserea I had no other thought than to see him again. I followed them in the train to Domnesti, about forty kilometers from Campulung, where there was a large cattle market. We stayed five days in all. He did conjuring tricks two or three times a day and they were never the same, and he changed the ceremony each time, too. He especially liked to do things in great style, real gala performances. The first day Lixandru appeared on a white horse, clothed like a prince, and he wandered all around the marketplace without uttering a word. I say it was Lixandru because I knew him and I'd talked with him in the morning. Otherwise I shouldn't have recognized him, because first of all the *Doftor* had changed him on that day. He'd made him taller and stronger, like a young man of twenty, and his hair was thick and fell in long locks down his back, the way men wore it in former times. And his face—although strictly speaking the *Doftor* hadn't changed it—still, it no longer seemed to be his face because he was much more handsome and he had a different expression—profound, noble, melancholy. How can I describe how he was dressed, and what a horse he rode? Everybody followed him—several hundred people—and stayed with him all the way to the *Doftor*'s tent. It was huge, such as only the big circuses in the cities were accustomed to use. How the *Doftor* carried it in the two carts in which he roamed through the villages I never understood. And there in front of the tent Ionescu was waiting for them, also transformed so you could no longer recognize him. He was tall and fat and black, thick-lipped like a blackamoor, dressed in full trousers, his torso naked, with a scimitar in his hand, and he shouted, 'Come in! We're working to get a dowry for Oana!' And when they entered the tent Aldea greeted them, seated at an elegant table with gold feet, surrounded by sacks of ducats. 'Five *bani*!* Five *bani*!' he shouted, 'but we'll give you change!' The people gave him five *bani* and received a ducat in change. 'But of course you know they're no longer good. They're not a medium of exchange, now,' Aldea told them, thrusting his hand into the sack and counting out the ducats.

"Great illusionist!" cried the man behind the desk.

"Very great!" Farama agreed. "I looked into the sacks of ducats. 'They're no longer a medium of exchange, *domnule* Principal,' Aldea said. And really, there were *thalers* from the time of Maria Theresia and ducats from Peter the Great, and many Turkish coins. But this was

*Smallest Romanian monetary unit: one *ban*.

44

nothing compared to what was to come. When the tent was full of people the *Doftor* appeared from behind a curtain in formal attire, with white gloves, with a mustache that was long and thin and very black. He clapped his hands and Oana came out from behind the curtain. She alone was just as I knew her to be. She seemed unchanged, though she was dressed differently, in a skin-tight white jersey. She looked like a statue. Then the *Doftor* raised his hand high and took from the air a little box no bigger than a pillbox, which he began to stretch so that it grew larger before our very eyes. He continued to tug it, now on one side, then on the other, on the bottom and on the top, until he made a chest of about two meters in length and approximately the same dimensions in breadth and depth. Then he took it and gave it to Oana to hold in both hands as high as she could reach above her head. Now, as Oana stood motionless, holding the chest up in the air with both hands, she resembled a statue more than ever. She looked like a caryatid. The *Doftor* stepped back and eyed her with satisfaction, then reached up again and took out of the air a box of matches. He removed some from the box and stretched them—lengthened them, broadened them—until he made a stairway which he propped against the chest. Then he turned to the audience and announced, 'Will the authorities please step forward?' And when no one ventured to approach he began to call them by name, as though he had always known them: '*Domnule* Mayor, please! *Domnule* Mayor, *doamna* Mayoress, bring Ionel with you, too. . . . And *domnule* Police Chief, please! Sergeant-Major Namolosu! And you come too, *domnule* teacher so-and-so. . . . ' In this way, one after another, he addressed each one and invited him to come out of the crowd. Taking them by the hand, he urged them to climb the stairs and enter the chest. The people were rather hesitant, but once they reached the top, in front of the door, they were ashamed to turn back and they went in. Thus the Mayor and his wife entered, and their son Ionel, the teacher, the Police Chief, and then the assistant to the Mayor with his whole family—he had come with three sisters-in-law, each with several children—and then the other people followed in no special order, as the *Doftor* invited them, calling them by name. About thirty or forty more went in like that, and finally he caught sight of the priest, who had just arrived, and stepping forward the *Doftor* invited him. 'Please, your Reverence, you come too. . . . ' At first the priest didn't want to. 'What kind of deviltry is this, *Doftore*?' he demanded. 'What are you doing to these people?' 'Come, your Reverence, and you'll see!'

"So the priest, who was old and walked with some difficulty—but was otherwise handsome and robust—climbed the stairs slowly and disappeared in the chest too. Oana had not moved in all this time. She might have been holding a kerchief in her hands. After he saw the priest enter the chest the *Doftor* climbed the stairs and began to manipulate it. He squeezed it, he pressed it, first on the sides, then from top to bottom, until it was reduced by half. Then he came down with it in his arms and in front of the crowd he again began to press it and make it more compact, and in a few minutes the chest had become what it was in the beginning—a little pillbox. Then he took it between his fingers, spun it around several times until he made it as tiny as a pea and

46

he asked, 'Who wants it?' And an old man replied from the back, 'Give it to me, *Doftore*, all my grandchildren are in it!' And the *Doftor* flicked it with his fingernail, but it was so tiny that as soon as he tossed it away, it vanished, and the next moment we heard a 'pop' and everybody— the priest and the mayor and all the others—were again in their places, each where he had been before. . . ."

"Terrific illusionist!"

"Unprecedented!" agreed Farama, nodding his head, "but this —what I just told you—is nothing compared with what happened at Campulung. There, at Campulung, the *Doftor* surpassed himself, for the whole garrison was there, the General and all, and their families; and because there had been a party that afternoon in the Public Garden, and the General had been satisfied with how it had turned out, he'd given the troops permission to come, too, as well as the military band, and the *Doftor* invited them all to enter the chest. But in my opinion it was a mistake to make the band play while they were climbing the stairs. They climbed up, blowing on the trombones and the other brasses, with the trumpeters in front and the drummers in the rear, until one last drummer reached the top. I don't know what happened to him, but he just stood there and beat his drum and didn't dare come back down. Then the *Doftor* motioned to him to stop and asked, 'What's the matter, soldier? Why don't you go in? Isn't there any room left for you?' 'There's plenty of room,' answered the drummer. 'There's no one in the chest. . . . ' The *Doftor* burst out laughing and raised his hand high, and the next moment they were all in their places, and the band played the regimental hymn. Then the General roared angrily, 'Who gave you the order to play?' And that's how it happened, at Campulung, that the *Doftor* couldn't stay until the end of the fair. . . ." Farama fell to musing silently.

"*Ei*, and then?" inquired the man at the desk. "What happened to Oana?"

"*Ei*, I was just thinking about that now," Farama went on, rubbing his knees in embarrassment, 'about how to tell you what ensued without going back and telling you about Lixandru and Darvari, and especially about their new friends whom they met at Fanica Tunsu's tavern—because it's a long story and in order to understand it you have to know what happened to Dragomir and Zamfira. . . ."

The man at the desk chuckled briefly to himself and pressed the button. "Good. We'll talk again."

The door opened and the youth with the radiant face reappeared.

"Thank you very much," said Farama, rising abruptly and bowing several times to his host.

V

THE VERY NEXT DAY FARAMA LEARNED THAT THE MAN HE
had been with was Economu, Undersecretary of State for
Internal Affairs. When Dumitrescu greeted him from behind his desk he spoke with somewhat more dejection
than previously.

"I've read another two hundred pages and still
haven't learned anything about Darvari. It's Darvari who
interests us, and only incidentally Lixandru and all the
others. The comrade Undersecretary of State Economu
has a great weakness for literature. He's enthusiastic
about Oana, but it's Darvari who interests us. When you
went to see Borza you intended to ask him about Lixandru. You didn't go to talk about Oana, so let's get back to
Lixandru and Darvari. You said a few days ago that
Lixandru had undertaken to teach Darvari the Hebrew
language. What connection does one have with the other?
Darvari had entered the Military School. Why did he
have to learn Hebrew?"

Farama felt intimidated. "He didn't have to, but as I
told you, it's a long story, and everything that happened
is related to Oana. You should know that Lixandru left
Bucuresti in the fall of 1916. He was in the retreat. When
he came back in 1918, a boy of sixteen or seventeen, he
entered the sixth grade at the *Liceu* Spiru Haret because
he'd taken private lessons in Iasi. A year later Darvari

49

entered the Military School at Targu-Mures. One day—I don't know what prompted him—Lixandru went to the rabbi on *calea* Mosilor and said to him, 'Probably you don't recognize me. I'm Lixandru, Iozi's friend, and I want to know what happened to Iozi, and that's why I've come to you. If Iozi had lived you would have taught him Hebrew long ago. I've come to ask you to teach it to me as you would have taught Iozi.' The rabbi didn't answer at once, but regarded the boy thoughtfully for a long time. Finally he said, 'Good. I'll teach you. Come here every morning an hour before you go to school and every afternoon an hour before sunset.' So that was how Lixandru began to learn Hebrew, and since he was an intelligent boy and industrious, when he took his baccalaureate two years later he knew it so well that he translated from the books of the Old Testament just as he would have translated from one of his poets. I forgot to tell you that Lixandru—who was a dreamer even in primary school and showed an inclination for poetry—read the poets all the time when he was in the *liceu*. But here, in poetry, he had strange tastes, too. At sixteen he read Calderon, Camoens, Sa de Miranda . . ."

"Leave this," interrupted Dumitrescu. "Tell me how he came to teach Hebrew to Darvari, and how Darvari, a pupil in the Military School with so many other things to study, agreed to learn Hebrew as well? What use would Hebrew be to him? Especially since he wanted to become an aviator."

"That's what gave Lixandru the idea, after Darvari told him he was going to be an aviator. 'Then you must come with me, too,' he said, 'to look for Iozi, and for this you'll have to learn Hebrew; because,' he added, 'you know, Iozi didn't die. If he had his body would have been found by now. He must be somewhere here on earth but we don't see him, or we don't know how to look for him; but eventually I'll discover how to look for him. . . . ' And so he proceeded to teach Darvari, giving him lessons only during vacations. But he bought him a grammar and a dictionary and made him study while he was in the Military School at Targu-Mures. However, I don't think Darvari tried very hard to learn. He hadn't Lixandru's memory nor his motivation. Then, too, there was something else. That year, 1919–1920, Lixandru and the boys had found Oana again and they went on Saturday evenings to Tunsu's tavern and took her out walking, not toward town but all around the outskirts of the city where everyone knew her, and the boys weren't shy about being seen with her. They walked like that across the fields until they came to the open country where the wheat farms begin. Oana walked among them singing, with her pigtails over her shoulders, and the boys accompanied her. But when on moonlit nights they stopped to rest among the weeds or under the mulberry trees, Lixandru would exclaim, 'Oana, I'm going to write a new mythology about you!' Of them all, Oana was fondest of Lixandru."

"Forget Oana," interrupted Dumitrescu. "I told you that we're interested first and foremost in Darvari's case."

"I meant to tell you about him, too," Farama smiled in confusion, "because during the vacations and especially in the summer of 1919 and Easter 1920, Darvari didn't miss the walks with Oana, Lixandru, and the boys, and a number of incidents had their origin in just such a walk. Perhaps that's why he didn't manage to

51

learn Hebrew very well. All the boys were between fifteen and seventeen and their great weakness was to return late, and after walking for hours to come back to have a bit of fun at Tunsu's tavern. Sometimes they came back so late—at two or three in the morning—that the innkeeper would go to bed as soon as he saw them come in, leaving the care of the inn to Oana and the musicians, unless they decided to leave too. It wasn't very often that a drunkard stayed late, and even so a scandal was avoided because everyone was afraid of Oana. So they— the boys—alone remained in charge of the tavern, and they had a wonderful time. All of them drank, but only moderately, and Lixandru hardly touched the wine although he was the most restless and high-spirited of all. He climbed up on the table and with his hand on Oana's shoulder, stroking her hair, he recited from his poets, especially the Spanish poets. No one understood Spanish, but they listened to him and watched him. Oana, though, was dreamy and absent, and often when Lixandru roused her she appeared to have been crying. And so it was that late one night, toward dawn, when he was reciting with his arm across Oana's shoulders, a couple entered the tavern. The young man was only a few years older than Lixandru, but he was very elegantly dressed and had a dark, handsome face with a provocative smile. He seemed a little dizzy when he came in, and hearing Lixandru reciting from Calderon, he exclaimed, 'How's this, aren't you Romanian?' But the woman just stood and stared at Oana and cried, 'It's she! It's my statue!' This woman who had come into the tavern was incomparably beautiful, but there was something wild and impetuous in her behavior and her clothing. She seemed eccentric, you might say, because she began at

52

once to clap her hands, approaching Oana as if she were a work of art, and she pulled off her bracelet immediately and held it out. 'A humble offering from Zamfira,' she said. That wasn't her name, the boys found out later, but she liked to call herself Zamfira, and although her cousin—the young man with whom she had come—was named Dragomir, she called him Dionis. These young folk, I learned later, had been through a great deal in their lives, but their families were descended from the *boier** Calomfir. And in order to understand what happened to them, and especially what is to follow, you have to know about the life of this *boier* Calomfir. . . ."

"Farama," Dumitrescu broke in sternly, "I've let you talk in order to see how far you think you can stretch the thread without breaking it. You're on to something. You keep rambling on and you think that if you can distract us with words, you'll get off more lightly. I told you to confine yourself to Darvari."

"But it's exactly about him that I'm going to tell you," explained Farama apologetically, "because for him everything started that night when he met Zamfira. I told you that this girl who called herself Zamfira was incomparably beautiful. Darvari was so astounded when he saw her that he fell in love on the spot as if he were bewitched. Lixandru spoke politely but very coldly to the newcomers and asked them, 'What do you wish?' Dragomir replied, 'I came to drink at the tavern, and she, the beautiful Zamfira, came to look for her model.' Lixandru said, 'We're sorry, but now when it's three in the morning, and God descends to earth, we like to enjoy ourselves alone.' Darvari motioned to Lixandru to let

*Nobleman.

53

them stay and then Zamfira noticed him. She came up to him, took his hand and said to him, 'Look! You see, he's a good boy and he wants us to enjoy ourselves in your inn, too!' Darvari became pale with happiness and excitement and he cried, 'I say let them stay, Lixandru! Maybe they have their signs, too!'

"The young man added with the same bitter smile on his lips, 'If you're set on hostility it doesn't really matter because it looks like I could beat you—all of you—but I'm afraid of the model and I'd have to fire the revolver, and who knows where I might hit her and then there'd be a scandal. . . . ' Oana began to laugh. 'I'm not afraid of bullets, *boierule*, because lead doesn't touch me. . . . ' 'But they're not lead bullets,' answered the young man, 'They're only caps with five different kinds of ink. . . . ' He took the revolver out of his pocket and showed it to them. It was just like a Browning but instead of bullets it had a powerful cap to make a 'pop!' and on the tip there was a capsule of colored liquid. 'I just got it from London,' added Dragomir. 'It can be useful for fashionable duels even in salons. It has bullets in five colors. . . . '

"So they stayed together that night and drank and had a wonderful time until the sun rose and the innkeeper woke up. When they left, Dragomir took a bundle of bills from his pocket and tried to pay, but Oana stopped him. 'After three in the morning when, as Lixandru told you, God descends to earth, you're all my guests. . . . '

"In front of the inn they found the carriage in which the young couple had come and they piled into it—as many as it would hold—and of course Lixandru and Darvari were among them.

"Soon after that a great friendship grew between Dragomir and Lixandru, and between Darvari and Zamfira. This girl was very strange. She didn't wear her hair like everyone else. It was neither too long nor too short, and sometimes she let it fall to her shoulders, sometimes to the nape of her neck. She didn't wear makeup, and she chose old-fashioned dresses, but she made them over in such a way that in the end they were like nothing else. Darvari was madly in love with her, and since he wore the uniform of a Military School, he thought it would impress her, but Zamfira told him . . ."

At that moment the telephone rang and Dumitrescu reached for the receiver, but he blushed when he heard the first words. "Yes, he's here," he said, and paused to listen. "Good, I'll do as you wish. I understand," he added presently and set the receiver in the cradle.

"Enough for today, he said to Farama. He appeared to be preoccupied, and the old man suddenly felt a great sympathy for him.

"You'll be questioned some more by other people," said Dumitrescu. "It's in your interest not to bring up the subject of Borza. Stick to Lixandru and Darvari. This Borza wasn't one of your pupils at Mantuleasa. He didn't go to any school, not even primary school. They discovered that for a long time he was a strong-arm man for the bourgeois parties in Tei and an informer of the bourgeois secret police. He had gained admittance to the Party by fraud. I think you understand me," he added as he pushed a button.

"I understand, and thank you very much," said Farama, standing up at once and bowing respectfully.

VI

THAT WEEK POLICE COMMISSIONER DUMITRESCU DID NOT
call him again to be questioned, but Farama continued to
write and the guard came regularly to get the finished
pages and bring him fresh sheets of paper. Then one
morning he entered the room and told the old man,
"Please come outside a moment, there's a surprise for
you. . . ." He smiled.

Farama laid the pen on the blotter, put the stopper in
the bottle of ink and stood up. In the passageway near
the door an elegantly dressed young man waited for him.

"Are you Zaharia Farama?"

"I am."

"Come with me. . . ."

They descended into the courtyard and crossed it,
going into another block of buildings and entering an
elevator. Farama noticed that the young man regarded
him with curiosity and kept smiling at him.

"I'm a writer too," he said when the elevator stopped.
"Your memoirs interest me very much."

They walked along several corridors before the young
man halted in front of a pair of massive doors, knocked,
and motioned to Farama to enter. The old man's shoulders were bent, as usual, his head a little bowed, but
when he caught sight of the woman who was looking at
him, smiling haughtily from the desk, he felt his legs
begin to tremble.

"Do you know me?" she asked.

"How could I not know you?" inquired Farama with a deep bow. "You are *doamna* Minister Anca Vogel. . . ."

"Comrade Minister," corrected the woman.

"The dreaded Anca Vogel," added Farama, trying to smile, "Everybody calls you that—the dreaded fighter. . . ."

"I know," said the woman, and she shrugged. "But I wonder why people are afraid of me. I haven't found out yet. I'm the milk of human kindness. I'm not tough except with my own, and not even with them. . . ."

For the first time Farama looked admiringly at her face. She seemed more fierce than he had judged from the photographs in the newspapers; a bulky woman with a broad, flat face creased by deep wrinkles; an enormous mouth, a thick, stocky neck. She appeared to be about fifty years old. Her gray hair was cut short in an almost boyish style. She smoked constantly, reaching across the desk to hand Farama a package of Lucky Strikes.

"Do you smoke?" she asked. "Sit down and have a cigarette."

Farama bowed again and sat in the armchair. Fearfully, he took the proffered package.

"There's a lighter beside you," said Anca Vogel. "You don't suspect why I summoned you," she went on, looking into his eyes and smiling. "I read a few dozen pages of your declaration. I couldn't read more because you're terribly long-winded and I don't have very much time to read, but I liked what you wrote. If you knew how to restrain yourself, to channel the torrent of your memories, you'd become a great writer. Only, you see, you don't know how to do that. You lose the thread and get stuck. I asked for all the passages about Oana to be extracted for me because I wanted to know her story from beginning to end, but I haven't yet managed to understand what happened to her. You're long-winded. . . ."

"Perhaps you're right," agreed Farama, nodding his head, "because I'm not a writer and I put down just what comes to me on the spur of the moment, but you can't understand the story of Oana like that, not by itself, because she wasn't alone in the world. She was the daughter of Fanica Tunsu and, above all, she was the granddaughter of the forester, and everything that happened to her—to Oana—was due to, related to, and fated by the breaking of her grandfather's agreement with the eldest son of the Pasha of Silistra . . ."

"Tell me this later," Anca Vogel interrupted. "I'd like to know now what happened to Oana after the war ended and she left for the mountains. When did this take place?"

"In the summer of the year 1920."

"Did you see her then? What was she like?"

"She was like a statue. She was eighteen and almost seven foot, nine."

"And was she beautiful?"

"She was beautiful as the statue of a goddess, like Venus. Her hair was reddish-blond and it fell over her bare shoulders—she always went around with her shoulders bare. She had breasts that were mature and firm, and you couldn't take your eyes off her. Her face was gentle and sweet like a goddess, with full red lips and intense black eyes that made you tremble. But what good were they? Because as I told you she was seven foot, nine. You didn't dare approach her. Like that, dressed, she scared you. If she'd run around naked you would

58

have become accustomed to her and you'd have said that she was built like a goddess, big everywhere . . ."

"*Ei!* Go on!" Anca Vogel encouraged him as she lit another cigarette.

"One day she went to her papa and said, 'Now, since the time has come, I'll go to the mountains, because that's where I'll find a husband . . . ' and she left. She took the train, but they put her off at Ploesti because some soldiers had molested her and Oana beat them up and put them all to shame. This girl had a Herculean strength, much more frightening than you'd have expected even from a giantess like her, a colossus of almost eight feet. I say that she shamed them because she pulled their pants down and spanked them in turn with her hand, like children, so they put her off the train at Ploesti. But she set out from there, going from village to village on foot, singing, with her knapsack on her shoulder, arriving in the Carpathians in less than a week. She stopped at the inns and bought her meals, because her papa had given her enough money, and then she set out again, singing, and bathing in the streams. She took off her dress and went in the water naked and without shame in broad daylight. The children from the villages followed her with rocks and set the dogs after her, but Oana didn't mind. She sang all the time and climbed up toward the mountains. In vain the shepherds' dogs chased her. She only turned around and motioned to them. '*Cutu, cutu!*' she said, and the dogs were quieted. They fawned on her, and capered about her. They seemed to have known her forever.

"And on the fifth evening after she left she reached a sheepfold below Piatra Craiului. The shepherds were

59

dumbfounded when they saw her approach, singing, with her knapsack over her shoulder and her feet bare. They set the dogs on her but Oana entered the fold with them fawning at her feet. She went to the old man, the chief shepherd, and said, 'If you'll let me live with you, *baciule*,* I'll work without pay. I'll do whatever work you give me to do, because I'm waiting for my future husband to come and get me here. . . . ' At first the chief shepherd didn't want to let her stay. He said he didn't need a monster of a woman on the mountain, but Oana spent the night in a nearby ravine and the next day she came again to the sheepfold and started to tidy things up, so the chief shepherd pretended not to see her and let her alone, and in the evening when all the shepherds came back with the sheep Oana invited them to wrestle with her—she was on her knees and they were on their feet—and she laid them all flat with their shoulders to the ground one after another. That week everyone in the mountains around there learned about Oana's coming and shepherds from the other folds came down—and they couldn't believe their eyes! At nightfall Oana went to the spring to bathe, naked, and the shepherds watched her from a distance. They couldn't take their eyes off her. The sight of Oana aroused them and they picked up courage and went one by one to the couch she'd made for herself, and they tried to possess her, but Oana rolled them over, each one, knocked them down, and went to bed immediately.

"One night five lads together tried to get the better of her. They attacked her while she was asleep and seized

*Chief shepherd (vocative).

her hands and feet, but it only woke her up and she tensed her arms and heaved up her waist, pitching into one after another until they fled with much groaning and howling."

"Formidable woman!" Anca Vogel smiled.

"Formidable," Farama repeated with a nod. "And after that they didn't dare come near her again. They only spied on her when she went to bathe, and they all followed her, aroused by watching her. When there was a full moon Oana went around naked with her hair falling down her back and she danced and capered and sang, and sometimes she put her hands together and prayed. But the shepherds didn't always hear what she said. Only once the old chief shepherd followed her, cowering behind the bushes, listening to her—and he was dumbfounded. 'Find me a mate, Great Lady,' she implored, raising her arms to the moon. 'Find me a husband my size, for I'm fed up with my virginity. God wronged me when he made me and then forgot me, but you, Great Lady, Lady Moon, Your Reverence—you look all around up there in the sky and you see near and far. Look well and find him for me! Bring me a man made to order for me and I'll take him for my husband in marriage!'

"And that night the chief shepherd made up his mind. He waited until the moon waned, since Oana didn't go out to bathe during the dark of the moon, and one evening he went to her. 'Oana!' he called. The girl woke up and approached him, but her steps were unsteady because she was still sleepy. Suddenly the chief shepherd struck her on the throat with a rawhide whip and Oana crumpled softly at his feet. He dragged her by

61

the hands to her couch and raped her. Then he went out and shouted to the shepherds in the fold, 'Come here!' And all the shepherds came and raped her in turn. When toward morning Oana wakened and went dizzily to bathe, she said to the chief shepherd, 'Thank you, *baciule!* This incident may be a lesson to me . . . ' And she began to laugh."

"Magnificent woman!"

"Formidable. But from this event came the chief shepherd's undoing, because beginning the next night Oana called the shepherds to her on her couch one at a time and she wore them all out by morning, and during the day the shepherds were sleepy. They could hardly wait to get away from the fold so they could sleep, leaving the sheep in the care of the dogs; but Oana went after them up on the mountain and whenever she found one sprawling in the shade she woke him and wore him out. The shepherds became rather reluctant to come at night, but Oana wouldn't let them alone. She knew them better now and she wasn't lenient with them. 'Who are you, *ma?*' she asked in the darkness, when the shepherd begged her to let him go back to the fold and get some sleep. 'I'm Dumitru,' replied the shepherd, and Oana said, 'But I haven't seen Patru this evening.' 'He's kind of sick,' said the shepherd. 'You go and send me Patru or I won't let you go until morning,' threatened Oana. Dumitru went to the fold. 'Get up, little brother, because if you don't come too, Oana will wear me out and I won't live to see morning again!' 'I'm too tired,' said Patru. 'Take Marin. . . . ' 'Marin was there earlier,' responded the other. 'You come. You're more rested. . . .' And so he brought him to her.

62

"In two weeks Oana had exhausted them all, and now the shepherds avoided her, hiding in the gorges and ravines so she wouldn't find them, so they could sleep, and in the evening they no longer returned to the fold except to bring the sheep. Several times Oana had come at night to the couch of the chief shepherd, but he'd anticipated this and slept with his whip beside him. 'Don't come near me, big girl,' he cried, 'I'm an old man and I want to see my children again so they can bury me at home in the village in the valley. Don't come near or I'll hit you.' And Oana pitied his age and forgave him. Then she set out at night on the mountain to find the rest of the shepherds.

"Soon this bad habit of Oana's became known to all the mountain people around and the other shepherds came, and Oana wore them all out on her couch, and in the morning they couldn't get back to their folds but fell asleep wherever they were. The sheep were left in the care of the dogs and they scattered, sliding down the slopes, bleating forlornly. All you could hear on the mountain was the dogs howling in the wilderness and the lamentations of the sheep, injured and godforsaken, and dying when they fell over the precipices. The people in the villages in the valley also heard about these goings-on and the eminent, arrogant men climbed up the mountain, and Oana received them in turn and wore them out, and on the second or third day they went down, exhausted and weary. Some of them didn't even reach their villages because they lay down along the edge of the road and slept, some even for a day and a night, as if they were resting after a serious illness. The women in the villages became frightened and it occurred to many that they'd lost their men completely, so powerless had Oana left them after they'd spent several days and nights with her up there on the mountain on her couch.

"Then the wives decided to put a spell on her—to make her dizzy and then to beat her, to trample her under their feet, to torture her. About fifty wives from all the villages in the valley climbed up there, and when they saw her—beautiful and naked, bathing in the spring, glancing over the cliffs and among the bushes to find a man who might have escaped her—the women were astounded and crossed themselves. Oana went to them just as she was, naked—only she'd gathered her long hair across her breast—and she asked them, 'What's the matter, good wives?' Then one of them stepped forward and said, 'We came to put a spell on you, big girl, to leave our men in peace, but now that we've seen you, it's no use to make a spell. You're not like us, wretched women, God's creatures. You're the seed of a giant. Mind you, you're descended from the Jewish Giants, the ones who tortured Our Lord Jesus Christ because they alone were big and powerful enough to do it even to him, the son of God. And if that's so, it's useless to put a spell on you, because it just won't take, but we beg you to let our men alone because they're not yours, and poor things, they're hardly any good to us, women with the fear of God in them. Go back where you came from. Look there for a husband like yourself, for it's only in the place where you were born that you'll find a giant lad you can marry, one who'll suit you in every way!'

"But Oana replied, 'Good wives, if I came to the mountain I did it deliberately, since it's this that's destined for me—to search for my man on the mountain—

and I was told also how I'd recognize him. He'll come down one day to me riding on two horses at once. . . . And if the chief shepherd hadn't struck me with the whip across the throat I'd not have known a man, because none of all the shepherds who tried to get the better of me had been able to defeat me; but then, like a thief, they made me know a man, and now it isn't my fault if I want to know them all. I'm not made of stone. . . . '

"'Big girl!' cried one of the women, 'a man riding on two horses you won't find around here, but you—if you're the seed of a giant—look for a *zmeu*.* Walk around the hills naked like you are and you'll see a *zmeu* jump up beside you. He'll be a match for you. . . . ' Oana looked at her for a long time and then smiled. 'Thank you, good wife, for these words you've spoken. They may be a lesson to me. . . . '

"And so it came about that Oana set out the very next day for a village in the valley. She put on the little bit of a dress that still remained and took her knapsack on her shoulder, thanked the chief shepherd and left, accompanied by the dogs for a good part of the way. Toward evening before she even came near the village, she spied a terrible bull way off on top of a knoll. The bull saw her, too, and he turned in her direction and lowered his head belligerently, preparing to confront her. He was a fierce bull, inconceivably fierce. A real bull. . . . Like in a story," Farama added with an embarrassed cough.

"Have a cigarette," urged Anca Vogel.

"Thank you very much," said Farama, bowing repeatedly. He lit the cigarette, and after he had inhaled the

*A kind of imaginary monster, dragon.

first smoke he smiled. "That's how it happened," he continued. "After that evening the bull never wanted to be separated from her. He stuck to her like a shadow and wouldn't let anyone come near her. It was the end of July and that summer was unusually hot. Oana flung away her rag of a dress and went about naked day and night, but on moonlit nights the bull bellowed loud enough to be heard in seven valleys and the people woke up terrified, and that's how they all happened to see her running naked over the hills with her hair floating over her shoulders and the bull behind her, and they'd see her stop suddenly, bend forward a little and shout when the bull penetrated her, and the two would remain there, joined together for a long time, the bull on her back, bellowing and striking sparks from his hooves. . . ."

"Formidable woman!" exclaimed Anca Vogel.

"Unbelievable!" agreed Farama. "But rumors of this bad habit of Oana's spread quickly through all the neighboring villages, and even reached Bucuresti, where the forester heard about it. He made the sign of the cross and said, 'Thank God that he's given me sufficient days to see the curse of Selim fulfilled.' And he went to the monastery, confessed and received the communion. 'Now,' he continued, 'although I'm rather old, God helping me, I may find me a young wife to start another line, because I'm no longer afraid of the curse. . . . ' The forester was a hundred years old but he was still robust, and that very fall he married a young widow of about thirty, but God didn't favor him again with a child. This widow, Floarea, was from Tiganesti, and she too had her story. . . ."

"Never mind the widow," interrupted Anca Vogel. "Tell me what happened to Oana."

"The authorities found out and the Legion of Police sent patrols over all the hills, and the people went out too with clubs and pitchforks—each with whatever came to hand—and at daybreak they came across her where she had made her couch, concealed by a precipice. From far off the bull came running to catch them on his horns and destroy them but the police shot and killed him. Oana said nothing. She covered herself with what remained of her dress and took her knapsack on her shoulder. When the police tried to put handcuffs on her she told them, 'Don't bind me! I'll come willingly.' And so she went down with the policemen, hooted at by the people but walking proudly with her head held high, smiling, her eyes turned to the east as if she were waiting for the sun. They hooted and shouted at her that she was a *curva** and wicked, and now and then she'd reply, 'It's not my fault. That's what the women advised me to do.'

"The sun had risen when they arrived in the village where the mayor and the chief of police were waiting, but they didn't take her into custody. Oana stood looking up the road in amazement. An unprecedented apparition was coming toward them—a hulk of a man, young, blond, astride two horses. Oana hurried to him and fell on her knees in the dust, seizing the horses by the bridle with both hands and bringing them to a halt. The policemen ran after her, but the man dismounted at once and lifted her out of the dust, and when the policemen saw how big and tall he was they all stepped aside. This young man was taller than Oana by a palm. He had a small beard, very blond, and he was dressed peculiarly, not like a countryman nor like a city dweller, either. He

*Whore, libertine.

took Oana's hand and approached the authorities. 'I am Dr. Cornelius Tarvastu,' he began, speaking Romanian, 'and I'm professor of Romance Languages at the University of Dorpat. I came here to study the dialect spoken in the Carpathians, but at a sheepfold I heard about Oana and I came down to get her. If you have no objections I'll make her my wife. . . . '

"Oana stood beside him and cried. The people didn't know what to do. No one dared to speak. Finally the mayor approached them and said, 'Good luck, *domnule* Professor, but don't have the wedding here!' 'That's why I brought two horses,' replied the Professor, 'so we can continue on our way.' But they didn't leave on horseback," added Farama, smiling, "because they were afraid the horses would collapse under them. They left on foot, holding hands, with their mounts walking slowly behind them."

"Formidable woman!" said Anca Vogel, musing. "And so they left Romania?"

"Not immediately. First Oana took him to Obor to introduce him to her father, the innkeeper, and they had the wedding at Paserea Monastery; but Oana brought him to Bucuresti especially to meet the boys, because she had also become fond of those new friends of Lixandru's, and what happened to them later came from this. Among Lixandru's new friends was that one Dragomir Calomfirescu—a strange boy, this one, too. . . ."

"Good. Tell me about this another time. Take the package of cigarettes with you," she added and pushed a button. "And if there's anything you want don't hesitate to tell me. . . ."

"I have only one request," began Farama, timidly.

"Give me permission to get some heavier clothes from home. It's become rather cold. . . ."

"Fine," said Anca Vogel, writing a few lines on the notepad in front of her, "Give this to the guard."

"Thank you very much," Farama responded, rising abruptly from the armchair. "And thank you, too, for the cigarettes. . . ."

VII

FOR ABOUT TWO WEEKS HE WAS NOT CALLED TO BE INTER-
rogated. The day after his interview with Anca Vogel they
had brought from home one of his old suits, a heavier
one. It had been raining for several days and the sky was
still half covered with clouds. Farama sat at the table and
wrote, bending over his papers, but he no longer scrib-
bled as rapidly and profusely as before. Sometimes he sat
for hours at a time resting his face in his hands, laboring
to remember if he had already written about a certain
incident or if he had only told it to Dumitrescu during
the numerous interrogations that had taken place previously, and because he did not always manage to recall
this he would write it again.

Then one night he was awakened at eleven o'clock.
"Get dressed," said the guard. His tone was more respectful than it had been on other occasions when he had
roused the old man for questioning. "Get dressed as fast
as you can. . . ."

Farama began to put on his clothes, but he was still
sleepy, and it was difficult because his hands were shaking. "It's gotten cold suddenly," he said, searching the
eyes of the guard apologetically.

"I wasn't supposed to tell you," the other whispered,
"but the car is waiting. Hurry. . . ."

All Farama's joints began to tremble then, and it was

not until he descended to the street between the guards, where he caught sight of the car, that he became more calm. Nothing bad is going to happen to me, he said to himself. Two officers in plain clothes climbed into the car with him without speaking.

"Autumn's here," murmured Farama after a while as if he were talking to himself, not daring to glance at the officers. "It's suddenly grown cold. There might be snow in the mountains. . . ."

In reply the man on his right held out a package of cigarettes and said, "Have a smoke. Perhaps it will warm you up. . . ."

"Thank you very much," Farama inclined his head several times in his customary manner. "I must say, I'd fallen asleep and was dreaming. I don't remember now what the dream was about, but the guard woke me up suddenly and the cold gripped me. That must be it—I jumped out of bed and was overcome by the cold. . . ."

Content, he smiled and lit the cigarette. After an interval of about ten minutes the car was halted by a cordon of police armed with machine guns. Some of them approached the driver. At once one of the officers put his head out of the window and whispered something, a few words that Farama could not understand. Then the car started again, proceeding slowly, and the old man kept catching glimpses of groups of armed police on guard in front of the houses. He realized that they had entered the quarter reserved for party officials and he began to tremble again. Still shaking, he got out when the car stopped. The entire street was brilliantly illuminated. He was led to a bolted door between two sentry boxes filled with police, where one of the officers rang the bell and spoke to someone. Finally the door was pushed open and they were allowed to enter.

In the lobby several policemen were waiting. Someone came up to Farama quickly and began to feel his clothes. He had not noticed the man at first because the chair on which he had been sitting was hidden among the policemen. Without speaking he beckoned to Farama to follow him and they climbed to a kind of loggia by an interior stairway, after passing through a spacious, well-lighted room. His guide motioned to him to remain where he was as he knocked briskly several times on a door. A woman's voice answered, "Come in!" The man seized Farama's arm, opened the door and pushed him inside.

"Good evening," said Anca Vogel, raising her eyes from the pile of papers which lay on the desk before her. "Come here and sit down. . . ."

Farama stepped forward anxiously, commencing to bow as soon as he reached the desk.

"Sit down and light up a cigarette," Anca Vogel suggested. The room was lined with elegant bookcases. On the desk there were several packages of Lucky Strikes, some ashtrays, and a large vase of flowers. Nearby on a small, low table stood two bottles of champagne, two glasses, and a bowl filled with fruit.

"I've had you brought here," the woman continued, "because at the Ministry I have too little time to listen to you, and then too I've more serious things to do there." She smiled. "I'd have liked for several of our writers to be able to listen to you—but this, perhaps, later. Meanwhile have some champagne to revive you. . . ." She picked up the bottle and poured him a glass.

72

"Thank you very much," said Farama, getting up suddenly to take it, bowing several times as he held it in his hand. "I see it's Veuve Cliquot champagne, and I haven't tasted it since before the war. I remember what the *Doftor* told me. *'Boier* Zaharia,' he said, 'whenever you happen to see or to drink Veuve Cliquot champagne, remember that it can change the fate of a man. . . . ' I knew what he was referring to," Farama added, sitting down again in the armchair and resting the glass on the edge of the desk. "I suppose I guessed it, but it was just the same as knowing, because what the forester failed to tell me I guessed anyway. This happened to him—the *Doftor*. His mother was a Greek woman from Smyrna and his father had an estate in the Baragan near Dor-Marunt. His mother was all for his marrying a Greek, too, one of her nieces, Caliope, also from Smyrna, and that's why she sent him home every Christmas—so the family could get to know him better. The *Doftor*, to the best of my knowledge, fell in love with Caliope and they even decided to become engaged. They were just waiting for the arrival of his parents from Romania, but eventually only his mother, the Greek, came because his father couldn't bear to leave Monte Carlo. On the evening of the engagement, the *Doftor*, who was now almost thirty and had traveled a lot, ordered Veuve Cliquot champagne. There was also at the engagement party an older friend of Caliope's parents. I don't know if he was Greek, too, or Armenian or whatever, but he was a man endowed with unusual powers. It amused him to do all kinds of tricks and sleight-of-hand in people's salons. When they were all clinking each other's glasses this old man went up to the *Doftor* and asked, 'But why didn't they give you pink

73

champagne?' The *Doftor* looked at his glass, and so did the others, and he saw that it was true—his champagne was pale gold in color, just like ordinary champagne. Caliope's family, who knew the old man well, said nothing. The *Doftor* asked for another glass and they poured out some more but it was still golden; and when they noticed that he became thoughtful and morose, they burst out laughing and said, 'This is just a trick of so-and-so. He's a great master illusionist. . . . ' And when the *Doftor* looked at the glass again he saw that it was full of pink champagne.

"'But how did you do it, *domnule*?' he asked, very curious. 'It's a long story and requires much training and great effort to master it,' the old man replied. 'But I'm eager to learn,' insisted the *Doftor*. 'It's too late now,' replied the other, joking, 'because tomorrow or the next day you're getting married and you won't have time to do anything but make love to your wife.' 'Well, no,' said the *Doftor*, 'we'll do just the contrary. You teach me first and later we'll get married. Caliope and I are both young and we can wait. We have plenty of time. Isn't that so, Caliope?'' He turned to his fiancée, but Caliope burst into tears and ran hastily out of the room. Her mama intervened and all the others protested in turn, but the *Doftor* wouldn't give in—first he'd learn to change the color of champagne and then he'd get married. . . .

"And that's how it happened that the *Doftor* didn't marry Caliope, although for a long time her mother did not lose hope, especially when her family compelled the old man to give him lessons. His teacher was astonished at the rapidity with which he learned all the sleight-of-hand and conjuring tricks. Caliope declared she wouldn't wait longer than a year, but he begged for another, and perhaps they would have been married anyway if Caliope hadn't fallen in love with another cousin who had just arrived from Greece, while he—the *Doftor*—met a Dutch sailor from the Far East and went off with him on his steamship. But poor Caliope suffered more from all these things because later the man she married became the confidential agent of a great ship-owner, Leonida, and there's a whole tale about him, too . . ."

"Farama," Anca Vogel interrupted, "drink your champagne and warm yourself."

Farama bent his head respectfully and drained the entire glass at a single gulp. Standing up, he bowed a number of times, placed the glass on the tray, and sat down again diffidently in the armchair.

"And now, before you get carried away with talking," continued Anca Vogel, "I want you to know that although I like to listen to all your stories, I'd like most to know what happened to Oana, to her husband—the Estonian professor—and to Lixandru. . . ."

"I'll get to this, too," Farama explained, smiling in embarrassment, "because at their wedding the *Doftor* told us about some of his adventures, and many other events are related to it, but in order to understand them you have to know that Lixandru had recently become friends with a young man somewhat older than he by about twelve years—Dragomir Calomfirescu. They liked to take walks at night on the streets, just the two of them, talking very little, because Dragomir was by nature silent and melancholy, and Lixandru, when he wasn't moved to recite verses, didn't talk much either. One night after they'd walked a long time in silence, Lixandru exclaimed suddenly, 'If I knew where the arrow went and where Iozi is *I'd know everything!*' Dragomir had only heard bits and pieces of these affairs, so Lixandru told him the whole story. When he finished, Dragomir smiled bitterly and said, 'In my childhood I wasn't lucky enough to have such strange adventures happen to me. Everything marvelous and extraordinary in my life happened before I was born, or long after my childhood was over. Even so I remember one detail, when I was eight and was admitted to the hospital with scarlet fever. They brought me all sorts of books full of adventure stories that I guess I read and forgot—except one by Carmen Sylva that I'll always remember, although I didn't get to finish it because the next morning I left the hospital and all the books I'd touched were burned, because they couldn't sterilize them in the autoclave. As a matter of fact I only recall some isolated fragments and maybe they're not significant—an incomparably beautiful girl who rode a white elephant, an old temple, a place in India. That's about all, but for me it's my childhood's most precious memory. For years I was tempted to search for the book and finish the story I'd started in the hospital, but I didn't do it and now I'm sure I'll never find out who that incomparably beautiful girl was or why she was riding a white elephant, and what she was looking for in a temple in India. . . . You,' Dragomir added, 'have learned Hebrew in order to understand a childhood adventure. It's good that you did, but be careful—*stop now!*' He stressed the words so strongly that Lixandru paused and asked, 'What do you mean?'

Dragomir took his arm and made him turn around. They were on Boulevard Ferdinand, a few hundred meters from the Fire Tower. 'Look behind you,' he said, 'to the third streetlight in front of the house with the white balconies. You see the house?' 'I see it.' *'Ei bine*, now come with me. It's not midnight yet, we still have time . . . ' and without adding anything more he took Lixandru by the arm again and started to walk rapidly in the direction of the Tower. When they reached it, he stopped and turned Lixandru to the right. 'How far can you see?' he inquired. 'Almost to the churchyard,' replied Lixandru. 'Good. . . . ' And they set out again, turning into Boulevard Pake Protopopescu and walking down Mantuleasa Street to Popa-Soare. 'Let's stop here,' said Dragomir. 'I know where there's a bench near here. We've time for a smoke.' They sat down on the bench and Dragomir took out his case and selected a cigarette. Lixandru waited impatiently for him to light it before he demanded, 'Well, what was this about?' 'All these places,' announced Dragomir, 'were once ours. They were all Calomfir's lands and now, except for the houses that you know, nothing is left to us because an ancestor of mine—one of Calomfir's grandchildren—wanted, like you, to find out about the people who lived under the earth—where they lived and how they lived.' 'I don't quite understand,' said Lixandru. 'Come with me and I'll explain it to you,' insisted Dragomir."

Farama paused and lit a cigarette. "You ought to know," he resumed with a smile, "that in those years there was on Popa-Soare an unusual cafe with a very special atmosphere. A linden tree hid the little garden in front. In summer a girl came there—not an extraordinarily beautiful girl, but a woman of charm. The men called her Leana, but she'd shake her head and respond, 'Don't call me that!' She wouldn't say more, because she had a weakness for surrounding herself with mystery. This girl, Leana, sang there and people came to hear her from the other neighborhoods because she knew old songs that others had forgotten, and she accompanied herself on a kind of lute—one that wasn't used anymore at that time. Dragomir took Lixandru to the tavern and they stayed there until almost morning. Leana sang only to them but they didn't listen to her because Dragomir was telling Lixandru about the life of Iorgu Calomfir. Now and then Leana would stop singing and listen, too, with the instrument on her lap. Dragomir would invite her to drink with them and she'd sit there listening with the jug of wine before her on the table. Sometimes she became thoughtful and she'd smile and stand up abruptly, lay the instrument against her breast and begin to play. . . .

"I'm telling you all this," explained Farama, embarrassed, "because this girl, Leana, had her story, too, and even though Lixandru never managed to find out how it ended, much that happened to him later was just because he met her that night when Dragomir took him to the tavern to tell him about the life of Iorgu Calomfir. You should know that this Iorgu Calomfir was Arghira's husband—the beauteous Arghira as she was called in her time, about 1700. This woman had been endowed by God with every blessing. She was so beautiful that news of her had spread across the Danube into Turkey, and she was still famous in Bucuresti almost a century after her death. The bands of gipsy musicians were singing about her even in 1850. And she wasn't only beautiful. She loved poetry and the theater—a rare thing for her time. She was educated, and she knew Italian, Spanish,

French, in addition to Romanian and Greek, but she had one great defect—she was very nearsighted and could scarcely see. Her father, the head of the village—and later her husband, Iorgu Calomfir—spent a fortune on doctors and oculists, bringing them to Romania from Stamboul or the West. In their homes, which were at that time somewhere between Boulevard Pake Protopopescu and Popa-Soare Street, there were always doctors and masters of lens-making. Some of them brought their little workshops with them and even installed a laboratory where they experimented with all kinds of glasses and lenses. Perhaps it was from one of these western masters that Iorgu first heard the legends and notions about crystals and precious stones concealed under the earth by some enchantment, things that can only be found with great effort and only by certain people. Maybe at first his great love for Arghira prompted this desire to know the subterranean world, and he may have said that if these beliefs were true, God might also help him to find the appropriate crystal that would restore Arghira's sight.

"But later unquestionably his wish to know about life under the earth became a ruling passion, because in the meantime—after Iorgu had built himself a sort of laboratory in one of the cellars and had begun making experiments, advised and aided by several foreign masters—in the meantime, I say, Arghira recovered her sight. How she recovered it is another story, but no doubt on that July night in the cafe on Popa-Soare, Dragomir didn't have time to tell it because Lixandru was impatient to find out about the predicament of Iorgu Calomfir, who had been overwhelmed by his passion for the subterranean secrets. After listening to all the legends and beliefs that the western masters told him about—how ores and gems are created under the influence of the sun and moon, how the veins of metal grow inside the mountains, and how they're guarded by elves and fairies, and other such tales—Iorgu remembered that at Easter the Romanian peasants toss baskets of red eggs into the streams, saying that the waters will take them to the country of the Good Folk, enchanted creatures who live somewhere under the earth, and they say the baskets bring the news to the Good Folk that Easter has come.

"And then he left the masters and miners of the west and began to wander about the countryside on his estates, questioning the old men and women, getting them to tell him everything they knew about the Good Folk and about their country under the earth; but they didn't know much more than everyone else knew—namely, that these Good Folk are kind and generous creatures, and that there under the earth they feed on men's leftovers and they pray constantly. It's known too that the Good Folk once lived on the face of the earth and that only after a certain event they retreated to the subterranean world. Now, Iorgu had formed the opinion that this belief concealed an earth-shaking truth, and that whoever succeeded in comprehending its meaning would not only find a place where it's possible to descend into the world of the Good Folk, but at the same time he'd understand all the other mysteries that the Church has not been permitted to reveal. . . .

"And then he returned from the country and shut himself for a whole day in his laboratory in the cellar, and had an iron door made and put a lock on it to be sure that no one would go down there without his knowledge.

What he did in his laboratory no one ever knew. Only one day a spring began to flow up into the cellar, and Iorgu ran outside in fright and ordered the men to bring buckets and pails and bail out the water. They worked day and night for a whole week, but the water came up with increasing force and Iorgu was so upset that he couldn't sleep. He stood at the top of the stairs, his beard in disarray, and shouted at them, 'Faster! Faster!' But it was all to no avail. After a week the water had filled the cellar all the way up the stairs. And then Iorgu raised his arm and cried, 'Stop! God hasn't helped me!' He was pale and thin and his eyes burned from weariness and lack of sleep. He dropped into an armchair, covered his face with his hands and began to cry, repeating again and again, 'God hasn't helped me!'"

Farama stopped and bowed, accepting the glass of champagne that Anca Vogel held across the desk for him. Then he lit another cigarette.

"Now," he went on after a pause, "I have to tell you that I learned all this the next day at school when I found myself in the staff room with Lixandru at noon. He entered hastily and he looked feverish, his eyes were so bright. He turned and looked at the door as though he feared someone was following him, and then he approached me. *'Domnule* Principal,' he began in a whisper, 'Please don't be angry, and don't question me, but I'd like you to let me go down alone into the cellar of the school. Don't laugh at me and don't ask me to tell you more,' he added, seeing my bewilderment, but the next moment the door was opened abruptly and a young girl rushed into the room. She hurried to me and seized both my hands. 'Don't let him, *domnule* Principal!' she cried.

'Don't let him go down into the cellar! Have pity on his youth!' 'But who are you?' I asked, trying to pull my hands from her grasp. 'How dare you enter a person's house without knocking?' 'If you knew everything I know you'd forgive me,' she said. 'Men call me Leana but that's not my name. God has punished me for my sins by making me sing in bars, but I wasn't meant for this, and now I'm singing at Floarea Soarelui,* here near your school. But last night I sang to them because I fell in love with them both the moment they came in, and I heard what the other one told him—the *boier*'s grandson, and I know the danger that's in store for him if you let him go down into the cellar. . . . '

"As he listened Lixandru turned pale. 'Don't pay any attention to her, *domnule* Principal,' he said. 'Leana's too panicky! She only sees dangers and enchantments. Make her go away and don't let her in another time unless she knocks properly at the door. . . . ' 'I don't understand anything!' I cried. 'Both of you sit down and tell me what this is all about. You begin,' I said, addressing the young woman. 'Don't listen to her, *domnule* Principal!' Lixandru interrupted, 'because this Leana, instead of entertaining the public, listens to their confidences and she doesn't understand them. . . . ' I turned to him at once with a sharp glance. He blushed but said no more. 'I couldn't sleep all night,' Leana began. 'After I realized what he intended to do I trembled because he's so young. I saw immediately that he's hot-tempered, and when I guessed what awaited him, I told myself that it's a God's pity that such a young boy should perish like that without his

*The Sunflower.

82

even beginning to know love, and since I couldn't sleep I waited for him on the street near the school. I knew he'd come and when I saw him going in I followed him, and please, *domnule* Principal, I pray to you as I'd pray to God, don't let him go down into the cellar!' 'But why?' I exclaimed, because I understood nothing. 'Let him tell you,' said Leana. 'I'll tell you,' Lixandru agreed, 'but only you. I'll tend to Leana later, but what I have to say now I'll say to you alone . . . ' 'I'll leave, *domnule* Principal,' Leana interrupted, 'but only if you swear that you won't let him go down into the cellar.' 'I can't do that,' I replied, 'because I don't know what this is all about, but you can be sure I won't let him go down there before hearing what else you have to say. Now be good and leave us alone. Go and wait for us in the garden. . . .'

"And that's how it was," Farama continued after a pause. "Left alone, Lixandru told me the story he'd heard that night about Iorgu Calomfir. It seems that after sitting for several hours in the armchair at the entrance to the cellar, watching the water continue to rise, Iorgu called his servant and questioned him. '*Chelarule,** how many in our family have died here?' He pointed to the rooms above the cellar. 'In these houses, *boierule,* no one has died,' replied the servant. 'Death came to *domnul* Calomfir at the vineyard, and the old *boieri,* your grandparents, died over there in the old house.' He pointed to the building opposite. 'God has addled my wits!' cried Iorgu, striking his forehead with the flat of his hand. Then he got up from the chair and said to the men, 'Don't worry, the water will go down. . . .' And it really did. That night

*Butler, steward, housekeeper (vocative).

83

it began to recede and within a week it had disappeared entirely. No one knew what was left of Iorgu's laboratory because as soon as the water stopped flowing he entered the cellar alone, closing the door behind him, and when he came out it seems that all he had in his hands was a little chest. The rest—whatever there was—he'd destroyed with his hammer.

"But soon after that he began to make experiments in the cellar of the old house. He ordered iron doors to be put up and stayed locked in there all the time, and after a few months the same story repeated itself. He ran up the steps shrieking for the men to bring buckets and pails, and they dipped out the water day and night until Iorgu motioned them to stop and buried his face in his hands again, discouraged. 'God isn't helping me!' he whispered; and yet a few months later he tried again the third time at the bottom of the garden where in times past there had been some houses that one of his ancestors tore down when he bought the property for a place to build his stables. Actually, under the stables were traces of a cellar and Iorgu installed his laboratory there. What happened after that I don't know because Lixandru didn't tell me, but no doubt he wasn't successful this time either, because before long he sold part of his property and went abroad.

"'Dragomir told me all this last night,' concluded Lixandru, 'but I didn't know that Leana was listening, too, and now I just ask this of you—give me permission to go down into the cellar. Because I don't know if you're aware of it, but the spot where the school stands belonged once to *boier* Calomfir.' 'This property and all these old houses,' I replied, 'were Mantuleasa's.' 'I

know,' said Lixandru, 'and I know too the story of how he got them, but it occurs to me that somewhere on this street, perhaps right where the school is, there are still signs.' 'What kind of signs, Lixandru?' I inquired. 'This—forgive me—and I can't tell you, *domnule* Principal,' said Lixandru, blushing. 'Very well, don't tell me.
. . . '

"I got up and so did Lixandru and we went out into the yard. As soon as Leana saw us she ran toward us, crying, '*Ei!* What do you say?' 'We'll all go down together into the cellar,' I answered. Leana fell on her knees and wound her arms around my legs, 'Don't let him, *domnule* Principal! Because it's a shame, he's so young!' 'Don't be afraid, little lady,' I pacified her, lifting her up, 'In our cellar there was never any water.' 'You've no way of knowing this,' Leana cried, but I was not impressed. I looked for the key to the cellar, took three candles— because there was only one bulb in the first room, at the entrance—and we went down. Leana stayed close to Lixandru, just a step behind and ready to catch him in her arms if any danger threatened. We walked around the cellar like that for more than a quarter of an hour. Lixandru was very pale, his lips tightly closed. He looked first at one wall, then at the other, bringing the flame of the candle close to the sand under foot, touching the walls with his hand, passing his palm slowly over them as if he were looking for who knows what signs. Then suddenly he turned to me and said, 'It's not here. We can go back.
. . . ' And then Leana hurried to him, took him in her arms and kissed him on both cheeks, crying, 'You're saved, *boierule!*' She took my hand and without any warning she kissed it. 'God give you luck, for your good

heart,' she said, and blowing out her candle she hastened up the stairs. . . .

"That's how I met Leana," said Farama, smiling. "That very evening I went to the garden Floarea Soarelui to hear her, and grew fond of her after that. Her story I heard later. I don't know what there was about the events that Dragomir related that might have frightened her, but I can say that all her rejoicing and kissing of Lixandru was premature, because the boy didn't calm down. The next day he began to go all over the neighborhood and ask for permission to go down into the cellars. Leana didn't find out about this until it was too late, and it would take many nights to tell you about all the things that happened to them both because of Lixandru's desire to inspect people's cellars."

"Take a break and drink another glass of champagne," said Anca Vogel, offering him the bottle across the desk.

Farama sprang excitedly to his feet and took it from her, filling his glass; then he went around the desk and replaced the bottle carefully in the silver bucket.

"Drink it now," insisted Anca Vogel, "or it will get warm."

Smiling and nodding, Farama sipped the champagne and unintentionally he sighed. He lit a cigarette and smoked for a few moments, musing, his eyes almost closed.

"Yes," he began suddenly, "this passion remained with Lixandru for a long time. He went to the houses all over my neighborhood and asked the people politely to let him go down into their cellars. Most of them chased him away and even threatened to turn him over to the police, but there were some who let him in, and Lixandru would go down into the cellar with candles and a pocket flashlight and inspect the walls, staying sometimes more than half an hour if he thought the moldy spots had been there a long time, revealing who knows what signs that only he would recognize. When he came out of the darkness his face would look paler, and he'd thank the people kindly and in payment he'd pause on the threshold and recite a few poems. He always commenced with Eminescu's 'Melancholy,' and if it seemed to him that the people in the house liked the verses, he's start to quote from the sonnets of Camoens, especially *Alma mintha gentil*. . . . He'd stand there on the threshold with one hand on his chest and the other resting on the doorframe, and he'd recite the verses. Most men misunderstood him, regarding him with bitterness and regret, because he'd become a handsome boy, and when they saw him standing in the doorway, pale, dusty, with the mold from the cellar on his hands, reciting Eminescu and Camoens, they closed their hearts to him even more. Many girls and maidservants fell in love with him, and the women sighed when they caught sight of him passing by on those same streets in the morning in late spring, or in summer toward evening, immediately after sunset. He thought people might be more amenable then and would receive him, whereas weeks and months before they'd driven him away and threatened to call the police.

"I saw him sometimes too from the staff room as he passed thoughtfully and sadly under the blossoming apricot trees. Near the school at that time," Farama smiled, "there were many apricot trees and on spring mornings they seemed to be covered with snow. When I had time I called to him, or even went down and talked with him on the street. 'Haven't you given up yet, Lixandru?' I'd ask him, smiling and teasing him, but right away he'd get excited and his eyes, deeper and brighter from insomnia, would pierce me with their gaze. 'If you knew what I know, *domnule* Principal,' he'd reply, 'you wouldn't be laughing. I learned a lot by questioning Dragomir, and I sense that the signs are somewhere here between the boulevard, Popa-Soare, and *calea* Mosilor,' and he waved his arm back and forth several times. 'If I had a billion I'd buy all these houses and tear them down,' he told me once. 'And you and the historians and archaeologists would be dumbfounded when you saw all the things I'd find here under the earth, beneath these sidewalks.' He pounded his heel in despair on the concrete. 'Human dwellings much older than you suspect. Not that they'd be of interest to me, because that's not what I'm looking for, but it would interest you—all of you—to find out how many secrets lie hidden underground, under these rocks and these houses. . . . '

"'Well, really, Lixandru,' I interrupted. 'You're a big boy now with book-learning. You're no longer a child. How can you imagine, at your age, that you'll find Iozi still alive after so many years, hidden underground? How *can* you believe something like that?' Lixandru's searching gaze rested on me for a long time and then he smiled sadly. 'I'm sorry, *domnule* Principal, that you think I'm a little touched in the head, or still have the mind of a child. I know very well that Iozi is alive, but not here and not underground, under our feet,' he added, pounding again with his heel on the sidewalk, 'but the signs I told you about must first be sought for under the ground. . . . '

"'What kind of signs, Lixandru?' I asked. 'You see,' he answered, smiling, 'I can't tell you this, because in order to understand the signs you must first recognize them. . . . ' He took leave of me then and went on his way under the flowering apricot trees.

"Sometimes I'd meet him at the cafe on Popa-Soare, where he'd go to hear Leana sing. He usually came in with Dragomir, but one time he came alone and he took me aside and said, 'It may seem strange to you, *domnule* Principal, but this Leana's harboring a great secret. Otherwise how would she too know the signs? Because I'm convinced that she does know them. Do you remember when she burst into the staff room after us? How else could she have suspected that it was so dangerous to go down into the cellar? You and the others weren't afraid. Why was she? This girl knows something. I listen to her sing, and it's often only to the two of us— Dragomir and me—and she comes over to us and smiles knowingly after a certain song. *After a certain song,*' he repeated, stressing the words, 'but how she happens to know it, and who taught it to her, she doesn't say.' 'What song, Lixandru?' I asked. 'Listen to her, *domnule* Principal, and you'll guess it. She sings it every night. . . . '

"And so it happened that I, too, took a great liking to the cafe on Popa-Soare and went there whenever I could to listen to Leana, until rumors began to circulate around the neighborhood that I'd lost my mind over her, but it wasn't true. I loved Leana as I loved so many others— adolescents and those in their early youth, the dreamers, the bold ones, and all who had something special, who saw something in life that was different from what we saw, we who were worn out and vexed with worries. But

I went more to listen to Leana, and because I'd grown to love the little cafe where she sang. I had a great weakness for all Popa-Soare Street because—you should know—this neighborhood of mine, Mantuleasa and Popa-Soare . . ."

Anca Vogel began to laugh suddenly. "No, Farama,' she said, pouring herself another glass of champagne. "Not that again, because morning's here. A little order in the memories. Tell me first what Oana's wedding was like and what happened to them afterwards—her and her Estonian. . . ."

"I intended to return to this," smiled Farama, "to Oana's wedding, I mean, but in order for you to understand what it was like you have to know that Dragomir's cousin, that beautiful and strange girl who called herself Zamfira, had taken a great fancy to Oana and came frequently to her father's tavern. Sometimes she came in the daytime, too, and brought her album and made sketches; but in order to understand what she wanted from Oana you have to know her story." Suddenly intimidated he stopped and glanced at Anca Vogel.

"The story of Zamfira!" she exclaimed, musing. "You say it's necessary to know Zamfira's story, too? How long is it?" she asked with a smile.

"Her true story," began Farama calmly, "lasts something more than two hundred years, because whatever happened to her started then, since she thought she resembled the other Zamfira, that girl I told you about who restored Arghira's sight."

Anca Vogel started to laugh again, "Farama!" She shook her head. "You're a strange man. . . . Put the pack of cigarettes in your pocket, you'll need it. Thank you for

90

this evening, and perhaps we'll see each other again. Good night!"

She extended her hand to him across the desk. Farama sprang abruptly to his feet, seized her fingers and touched them lightly with his lips.

"Thank you very much," he said. "Thank you very much for the cigarettes and for your trust. . . ."

VIII

HE CONTINUED TO WRITE EVERY DAY, BUT NOW HE WROTE with great care and deliberation, rereading the pages with concentrated attention before entrusting them to the guard. He knew that he kept returning involuntarily to the events that seemed essential to him, but he was not worried about the inevitable repetitions. Instead, he was concerned because of the confusions which might arise from variations of the same narrative presented in different perspectives. Farama had realized this when, after many weeks, he again found himself summoned to Dumitrescu's office.

"It could be said that I wish you well," was Dumitrescu's greeting, "yet I also wonder why—because I'm not a writer, and I haven't lost my mind over artists and writers like so many others around here. Perhaps you understand," he added with a bitter smile, "that your stories have passed through many hands, and even people of great responsibility have read them, not to mention numerous writers of note, young and old."

"I didn't know," faltered Farama, his face red. "I didn't know that . . ."

"You'll know it from now on," Dumitrescu interrupted, "but I want to call to your attention that as far as I'm concerned the literary value of your statements is not important. I'm interested solely in the progress of the investigation and I want to talk to you about this. In the many—too many—hundreds of pages you've written up to now, and in all the verbal declarations you've made, the relation of Lixandru and Darvari hasn't yet been made clear."

"In the primary school they were friends . . ."

"I'm not talking about primary school," Dumitrescu broke in, "and not about their friendship with Oana, either, or Zamfira, and all the others. I'm talking about their relationship in 1930 when Darvari took off in the plane and disappeared in Russia."

"They were friends then, too . . ."

"This isn't clear from your statements, and it isn't clear because—at least it would seem so at first sight— you contradict yourself. In a moment I'll show you some quotations and you'll see, too, that you're confused and you sometimes contradict yourself. . . . Maybe I shouldn't tell you this," he went on after a pause, "but maybe unconsciously I wish you well. I wonder—do you contradict yourself because you no longer remember in detail how things happened, or because you're trying to *hide something*? If you really want to hide something, all I can tell you is that you delude yourself, and it would be sad at your age to be still deluding yourself. . . ."

They were both silent for a few moments.

"I understand," said Farama, forcing himself to smile. "I understand and I thank you very much. I'm not trying to hide anything, but I know what you're referring to. When things aren't told as they ought to be told they sometimes appear confused, and *some of the details seem to contradict the whole*, as I would have said in school. For that reason I'll be as careful as possible from now on, and I'll write as clearly as I can."

"It's in your own interest," said Dumitrescu, reaching

93

for the button. "By the way," he added, searching the old man's eyes, "I can tell you something you probably had no way of knowing—Darvari never reached Russia, and the plane in which he fled was never found, either, although they made extensive inquiries, the Russians and Romanians, both. I think you understand what this means. . . ."

That day Farama wrote almost nothing. He sat for a long time with his hands at his temples, the sheets of paper before him on the table; then with sudden decision he started to note down the dates—1700 (Arghira), 1840 (Selim), October 1915 (Iozi), Autumn 1920 (Oana's wedding), 1919–1925 (Marina-Darvari), 1930. . . . He stopped and considered the entries absently, crossing them out finally one by one, carefully and meticulously, dipping his small pen in the ink at frequent intervals.

The next day he began to write again as concisely and clearly as possible about the events of the years 1914 and 1915 up to Iozi's disappearance. Every day after that he outlined in the dry style of a bureaucratic report the sequence of events that had immediately preceded the afternoon when the rabbi's son vanished, all of which had some connection, direct or otherwise, with Mantuleasa Street.

After about a week the guard again woke him. "Please, the car is here. Please come for a drive." He smiled.

They reached the villa almost at midnight and he found Anca Vogel seated at the desk, smoking, with a pile of folders before her, the two bottles of champagne on the little table nearby.

"Good evening, Farama," she called. "Come sit down

and light up." She held out the package of Lucky Strikes across the desk. "Rest a moment and have a glass of champagne," she added, picking up the bottle and filling the glasses.

"Thank you. Thank you very much," repeated Farama, inclining his head several times.

"And after you've rested continue your tale, although not in the way you like to talk, haphazardly, but be selective, if you know what I mean. From everything you know choose the most significant parts. For instance, this evening, Oana's wedding."

"If you'll permit me, I'll begin with the story of Zamfira . . ."

"You said it covers two hundred years," Anca Vogel interrupted, smiling.

"I'll condense it as much as I can, but without knowing what happened 200 years ago and more, you won't understand Oana's wedding and what occurred after that."

Anca Vogel smiled again, shrugged, and filled her glass with champagne.

"Maybe you remember," began Farama, "that the wife of the *boier* Iorgu Calomfir, the beauteous Arghira, as she was called, had very weak eyesight. Although she wanted to read and loved books, she couldn't actually read them with her own eyes. She just took them in her fingers, stroked them, brought them close to her face so she could decipher the titles, and then she gave them to her companion, a Greek woman, to read to her.

"In addition to poems and novels and all kinds of travel books, Arghira liked the theater. She had a real passion for it. As soon as she married Calomfir she begged him to break down the wall between two large rooms and to replace it with columns and build a theater for her. Still, although she would have liked to act she was too nearsighted and had to be content with dressing her friends and her friends' children in costumes made according to her designs, letting them do the acting. She liked to create garments in bright spectacular colors, and she herself selected the materials, the velvets and silks, choosing colors that she could see—flaming red velvets and silks white as snow, stuffs that were threaded with gold, and different silks from Turkey—green, blue, orange. When the actors put on their costumes she went up to them and felt them in order to know if they'd been sewn as she had directed, but she could see the colors even without coming near them. When the play began, she sat in a comfortable chair right in front of the stage, and she followed the text easily because most of the time she'd memorized it.

"Her husband, as I've told you before, had spent a fortune on doctors and master opticians, but it was in vain that they brought her all kinds of spectacles, because as soon as she put them on her eyes began to water. Not a single doctor had managed to discover the reason why Arghira's eyes couldn't endure any kind of lens. Various quacks and healers came, and in turn they tried their charms and remedies, but all without success. Until one Sunday morning, after mass, a young girl from another village climbed the stairs to Arghira's room in the tower and said, 'I am Zamfira. Wash your face with this water and God will give you back your sight. . . . ' And strange as it may seem, that's what happened. Arghira washed her face with that water and she could see just as other people see. She embraced Zamfira, giving her gifts and begging her to come every day to see her in the tower. Soon after that Arghira found a husband for her— Mantuleasa, a confidential agent of her father's—and she gave her friend the houses and the lands on which Mantuleasa Street was later laid out, but this is another story and perhaps I'll tell it to you on another occasion. . . ."

"What I wanted to tell you now," he resumed after lighting another cigarette, "is that Dragomir's cousin, the sculptress—her real name was Marina—had learned when she was a child about all these events that I'm relating to you now, and it seemed to her that Zamfira was in her way a saint, and she thought, too, that she—Marina—resembled Zamfira and that perhaps she might even be Zamfira returned to earth after two hundred years—not to give back Arghira's sight, but to teach people *how to see*. Because, she thought, people no longer know how to see, to look around them, and all the evils and vices derive from this—that in our day people are almost blind; but there's no other way to heal them except to teach them how to look at works of art and, above all, sculpture. That's why she had such a great weakness for Oana and came so often to Tunsu's tavern to draw her. She filled whole albums with sketches, claiming that only Oana was fit to serve as a model for a goddess."

"No, Farama," interrupted Anca Vogel, raising her head abruptly. "All this doesn't interest me. I asked you to tell me about Oana's wedding."

"We'll get to that in a few minutes," said Farama, blushing. "Because Marina was also at the wedding at Paserea Monastery, and so were all the others, her friends and Oana's."

"When was the wedding?"

"In the fall of 1920."

"And all you just told me about Marina who called herself Zamfira—when did this happen?"

"About a year before, during 1919."

"Well, leave this and come directly to the wedding."

Farama bent his head and began to rub his knees nervously. "If that's what you want, that's what I'll do. I'll just ask for a few more seconds to mention briefly that Marina had hardly begun to work on the *Birth of Venus* when Oana asked permission of her father to go to the mountains and left. So that summer Marina was without a model. In despair she gathered the boys at her home, partying night after night. I must tell you that none of them had ever entered such a rich and noble house before."

"Those few seconds are long gone," Anca Vogel interrupted, smiling at him.

"Forgive me, but it's curious that I can't skip certain details which at first sight seem unimportant, yet are nevertheless decisive for what will happen later. It was necessary to recall this old, rich house because Marina's aunts lived there, two old women whose minds seemed to have been failing for a long time, but only *seemed* to, actually . . ."

"*Ei*, and what's that got to do with it?" Anca Vogel spoke rather sharply.

"It has to do with it because these old ladies kept telling the boys—although you realize that at that time, that summer, not one of them was yet twenty—they told them, 'Don't fall in love with Marina because she's destined for Dragomir. She has to marry him; otherwise, the line will die out. . . .'"

He stopped suddenly, frightened not so much by the telephone, which had started to ring, as by the abrupt change that he had glimpsed on the woman's face. Anca Vogel frowned at him and nervously extinguished the cigarette she had scarcely begun. Then she raised the receiver to her ear with a strained smile. Farama began to feel frightened and turned away, looking at one of the bookcases. "Good," he heard her whisper, then after a pause she hastily added a few words in Russian and replaced the receiver in its cradle.

"Farama," she began in a voice that seemed changed, "You're a lucky man." She filled her glass with champagne, drank it up and lit another cigarette. "But I don't know if you bring luck to others, too. We'll see about this later." She smiled absently. "In any case it could be even more mysterious than you suspected when you started to invent these tales of Oana and Zamfira."

"I give you my word of honor," whispered Farama, turning pale.

"Please don't interrupt me. It's all the same to me whether or not the adventures you've written about and told are all invented, but it poses a slight psychological problem and I'd like to know how to resolve it. It poses this problem—why do you invent this world as you go along? Is it simply because you're afraid and hope that in this way you'll be able to get off more easily? But then I don't understand *why you're afraid*. I don't understand what danger you want to *escape*. . . ."

Farama's face turned white and he stroked his knees mechanically, but he did not dare to say anything more although Anca Vogel regarded him with curiosity for several moments as if she were waiting for a response.

"Anyway," she resumed after filling her glass again, "you're a lucky man because you don't suspect the surprise I'd prepared for you tonight. You don't even dream of it!" she added, managing a smile. "A limousine is waiting outside and I'd intended for us to take a drive after three o'clock—when according to you, God descends to earth—to drive together on Mantuleasa Street, so you could point out to me your school, and the taverns, and the houses with the deep cellars . . ."

"You should see it in summer!" Farama burst out suddenly with unaccustomed fervor. "You should see it when the trees are loaded with ripe cherries and apricots!"

The woman gazed at him again profoundly, and musing, she began to sip her champagne. "But as I said, you're a lucky man. I'll never know if you invented these tales, or how many you invented, because it's no longer possible to drive on Mantuleasa Street. . . ."

She stopped and burst into laughter as Farama sprang to his feet in fright. "More precisely," she continued, "one can't go there tonight—or at least we can't—we two. So you see, things are even more complicated than your stories would imply. . . ."

She pressed the button as she spoke the last words and in a moment the guard entered. "Give him some cigarettes," she said, "and get him in the car quickly."

Standing up abruptly she hurried to the opposite end of the room where through the curtains a balcony could be seen. Farama bowed deeply with effort, trying to control his trembling. He felt the agent's hand on his arm and allowed himself to be led away without resistance, but when he arrived in the courtyard and saw a group of

100

men clad in long cloaks waiting for him, not a familiar face among them, he felt his legs give way and would have fallen if the guard had not supported him.

"What else did she say?" asked one of the men, with both hands deep in his overcoat pockets.

"She said to give him some cigarettes."

IX

HE FOUND HIMSELF SEATED ON A CHAIR IN A ROOM THAT
was lighted insufficiently and strangely. All he could see
was the desk in front of him, and behind the desk two
strangers staring at him absently.

"Please excuse me," he began, after glancing around
in amazement. "I was very tired. I don't know very well
how I got here. I'd had the honor of being invited by
Comrade Minister Anca Vogel . . ."

"It was exactly with regard to this that we wanted to
ask you a few questions," one of the men interrupted. He
had thin hair that was stuck carefully to the top of his
head and he was wearing dark glasses. His hands were
clasped on top of a file folder on the desk before him.
"First of all," he continued, uttering the words slowly
and weightily, "I'd like to know if Comrade Vogel said
anything to you about Economu."

"About the Undersecretary of State for Internal
Affairs?"

"He's no longer Undersecretary of State. We want to
know if Comrade Vogel said anything to you about Vasile
Economu. Try hard to remember," he added, smiling,
when Farama shook his head vigorously. "It's very important and it will considerably alleviate your situation.
. . ."

At that moment the other man held out the package

of cigarettes and the lighter. He had only a few yellowed teeth which he kept revealing in a forced, melancholy smile. Farama took a cigarette and lit it quickly, trying to quiet the trembling of his hands.

"I can assure you that never, in the conversations I was privileged to have with Comrade Minister Vogel, never did I hear her mention the name of *domnul* Economu."

"And yet you were summoned to Comrade Vogel after you had a long discussion with Vasile Economu, who was at that time Undersecretary of State for Internal Affairs."

"I couldn't say that I had a long discussion," protested Farama after drawing deeply on the cigarette. "In fact, I don't know if *domnul* Economu had the opportunity to utter more than a few words. He wanted me especially to tell him something about Oana, the daughter of the tavern-keeper at Obor. I told him and he listened to me."

"We'd like to know this, too," the man with the dark glasses interrupted again, "why, *after* you told Economu certain things about Oana, Comrade Vogel called you to come and tell her about them, too? Or, perhaps," he added after a pause, gazing intently into Farama's eyes, "perhaps Economu had let it be understood that there were *other* things to be discovered about Oana, things that could interest Comrade Vogel *directly?*"

Farama looked down. "What kind of things? What things could have interested Comrade Minister Vogel in an old story that she didn't even believe, that she suspected was invented by me?"

"How do you know she didn't believe it?"

103

"She told me so herself this evening—or whenever it was—actually last night, when I was with her the last time. . . ."

"But when did she admit to you that she didn't believe you? Before or after she was called on the phone?"

Farama's face went pale and he put out his cigarette uneasily in the ashtray. "After," he whispered, "after she spoke on the phone."

The two men glanced at each other without smiling. "Of course, *after*; but until then she hadn't shown a sign of doubting the truth of the story, and it's just this that we want to know—why, after Economu found out about Oana's story, did he believe that *certain* things, or perhaps only *one* certain thing, in connection with this tale could interest Comrade Vogel directly? Or, to be more precise, try to remember if, while telling Economu about Oana's adventures you told him also about her wedding at Paserea Monastery—in other words, if you related to him Oana's dream, the dream she told you at the Monastery."

Farama brought both hands to his temples and sat for some time without moving. "As far as I can recall," he whispered, "I had only started to tell *domnul* Economu about Oana's adolescence and the adventures with the *Doftor*, when she and her friends accompanied the *Doftor* on his travels to the market towns in the mountains."

"That is," the man with the dark glasses broke in, opening his file, "the events of 1916."

"Precisely. Summer, 1916, before Romania entered the war."

"And therefore, things that don't interest us. It's useless to dwell on them. Let's go back however to Oana's wedding. Can you describe for me the reaction of Comrade Vogel at the time you were telling her about Oana's wedding?"

Farama smiled. "All I can tell you," he began, his spirits rising, "is that unfortunately I didn't get to tell the Comrade Minister about this fabulous wedding in spite of the fact that she asked me this herself several times, and she was rather insistent. And this wasn't because I didn't want to tell her, but I've said a number of times—not only to Comrade Minister Vogel—that in order to be able to understand what Oana's wedding meant to her and all her friends, it was necessary to know first—on the one hand—all that had happened about a hundred years previously, and on the other hand, what happened a hundred years before that."

"Be more explicit," interrupted the man with the dark glasses, leafing carefully through the file. The other handed Farama the package of cigarettes again and smiled at him.

"I was referring to the story of Selim," said the old man after he had lit his cigarette, "and the story of the *boier* Calomfir."

"You wrote about them several times but the connection between them isn't clear. Here's what you wrote. I summarize—in 1835 Selim, the son of the Pasha of Silistra, saves the life of a boy of about fourteen or fifteen and the boys bind themselves to each other like brothers. Selim is married when young to a Turkish girl and a Greek-Turkish girl, but very soon he discovers that his friend deceives him with both wives and he curses him. The friend changes his name to Tunsu, flees to Ardeal and from there into Muntenia. This happened in 1848.

105

Tunsu loved women and was in great demand with them but he was afraid of marriage; and so it went until 1870 when he reached the age of fifty and married a widow with three children. . . . I don't see any connection with Oana's wedding," he added, interrupting his reading.

"And yet there *is* a connection. Perhaps I didn't write it clearly enough, but you see this was the curse of Selim: Because his best friend had betrayed him—the man whose life he'd saved—he cursed him so that in his family all the wives would leave their husbands and their daughters would mate with beasts—and that's what happened. Tunsu married at fifty, but after their only child, Fanica, was born, the wife ran off with a farmhand. After that Tunsu lived alone in the forest near Paserea Monastery. His son, Fanica Tunsu, becomes an innkeeper in Obor, marries and has Oana, but his wife leaves him too. Folks say she left him and ran away after she saw how amazingly large Oana was growing and she'd found out from her husband about Selim's curse; but Oana, poor thing, although she was well-behaved and unacquainted with evil, fulfilled the curse, too, because finally—but perhaps you too know the story . . ."

"We know. And in connection with this tale— because very probably that's all it is, something the mountain men made up, or maybe their wives—in connection with this story we'd like you to relate to us the reactions of Comrade Vogel. What did she say? What comments did she make? Do you recall anything else?"

"She exclaimed several times as she listened to it, 'Formidable woman!'"

Wearily the two men looked at each other again with blank faces. "Let's go on now to the other point, still in relation to Oana's wedding. You also said that the other story, about Calomfir, which began around 1700, would be just as important; but from all you've written and declared verbally this doesn't follow."

He opened the file again, took out a typed page and running over it hastily, continued very slowly and deliberately. "It was hard to summarize the stories connected with Calomfir because you've jumped constantly from Arghira and Zamfira, the girl who restored Arghira's sight at the beginning of the eighteenth century, to the sculptress who wanted to call herself Zamfira although her name was Marina, and who, if she were alive today, from what you say, might be sixty years old—sometimes ten to fifteen years less, sometimes more. Because," he added, raising his eyes from the page and looking at Farama with well-stressed irony, "however exact are the majority of the dates in connection with the characters of our times or in other centuries, Marina's age varies in your statements in an almost spectacular manner."

"It's true," said Farama thoughtfully. "For me this woman, Marina, has remained to this day a mystery."

"We'll get back immediately to this mystery and perhaps we'll clear it up. I said that it's hard to summarize this Calomfir cycle because you jump constantly from one century to another. You jump from Calomfir and Arghira to Dragomir and his cousin Marina and there's only a casual reference to Mantuleasa. . . ."

Without realizing what he was doing Farama began to rub his knees nervously.

"All you've said—and you've repeated it several times—is that Arghira married Zamfira to a man from her father's estate, Mantuleasa, and she gave them the land where the street with the same name was later cut through. Is it possible for you to recall so little about *this* family, which was so much closer to you than the family of the *boier* Calomfir and Dragomir Calomfirescu?"

"I never knew very much about the Mantuleasa family," Farama said apologetically, lowering his eyes. "You see, for me, only the school mattered and what was around the school—the houses, the gardens, the cafes with their summer gardens. . . ."

The two men regarded each other in silence. The one with the few yellowed teeth smiled sadly, shrugged, and again offered the package of cigarettes to Farama across the desk.

"Let's leave this, then, for a moment," resumed the other, looking over the typed page absently. "Let's go back to Oana's wedding. . . . But before this I'd like to ask you something else, also related to Mantuleasa. When you saw Comrade Vogel for the last time did she say anything to you about Mantuleasa? Or perhaps about Mantuleasa Street?" he added after a brief pause.

A dreamy smile lit Farama's face. "She not only said something," he stated with a pride that he could not well conceal, "but she had even prepared a surprise for me, namely this: For both of us to ride in the limousine after three in the morning on Mantuleasa Street. She wanted to discover its charm for herself. . . . Of course I told her that now on the threshold of winter there wasn't so much to be seen. I invited her to come and look at it when the apricot trees are in bloom, or when the cherries are ripe and the apricots are beginning to turn red."

The men looked at each other with interest. They

seemed almost disturbed. "And yet you didn't go riding," the one with the sunglasses commented presently. "Why? What explanation did she give you?"

"She told me we couldn't drive on Mantuleasa Street that night—at least the *two of us* couldn't. . . ."

"Of course she told you this after she was called to the phone, and she didn't add anything else?"

"No. Nothing else."

"Good. Let's return, then, to Oana's wedding. There are two things that interest us especially—the dream that Oana told at that time, and the curious behavior of Marina. The three successive narratives, only a few months apart, present considerable variation. Let's begin with Oana's dream that you just mentioned," he added, raising his eyes from the page and looking pointedly at Farama, "You stated that *you didn't tell it to either Vasile Economu or Comrade Vogel.* Before analyzing it I'd like you to tell us once more about this dream as precisely as possible and with all the details you can remember, because for us it's the details that count. . . ."

Farama sighed and wearily rested both hands in his lap. "Only the dream?" he asked in a whisper. "And not what happened before?"

"Only the dream. What happened before is of less interest."

Farama gazed into space for a few moments as if he were trying to remember. "It happened like this," he began suddenly. "On that night—that is, the Saturday before the wedding—Oana had this dream which she told us about at the feast on Sunday evening. We were all seated around the table. On her right was the bridegroom, the Estonian professor, and on her left, her father;

and suddenly she exclaimed to Lixandru, 'Listen, Lixandru, listen to this, and interpret my dream. It seemed,' she began, 'that I was swimming in the Danube, but I was swimming up the river and after some time—I don't know how long—I came to the spring, the source of the Danube. And there I discovered suddenly that I'd penetrated into the earth, into an endless glittering cavern with walls all set with jewels and lighted by thousands of candles.

"'And a priest who was there with me whispered, "It's Easter. That's why they've lit so many candles." But I heard at that moment a voice from an invisible source. "It is not Easter here, because in this land we are still in the Old Testament." And I felt a great joy as I looked at all the candles and the lights and the jewels, and I said to myself, "I too have been privileged to understand how holy the Old Testament is, how much God loved those people who lived in Old Testament times." And then I woke up. . . . ' This was the dream Oana told us."

"Go on," urged his interrogator, seeing that Farama was silent, "because what comes now is equally important."

"Go on . . ." repeated Farama thoughtfully. "Many more things happened that night."

"We're interested to know down to the last detail the reactions of Lixandru, Darvari, and Marina."

"That's where I thought I'd begin," agreed Farama. "I was seated next to Lixandru and I was struck first by his pallor and then by his agitation. He sprang up from the table as if he had been stung and hurried to Oana, seizing her hand. 'The signs were revealed to you, too!' he exclaimed. 'They were revealed in a dream. This is the cavern under the water that I saw too, long ago, and Iozi's living there now. If you hadn't wakened you'd have met him! And maybe he'd have said something for you to tell us—how to find the passage the second time!'

"Then he seemed to realize that he ought not to have said all this right there at the wedding in front of so many people, and he became confused and apologized, and returned silently to his place beside me; but he couldn't avoid Marina, who'd been listening spellbound and called to him from the other end of the table to explain the signs to them. Seeing that Lixandru remained silent, Marina smiled happily and went to him, catching him around the waist. She kept him with her all night, even though she saw that Darvari was annoyed; and there were many who thought that night that the friendship between Darvari and Lixandru was broken, but this wasn't true. . . ."

"We'll hear later your explanation of why it wasn't true, although according to your own statement it was quite the contrary," the man with the dark glasses suggested. "For the moment I'd like to emphasize this— in all three versions that we have in the file and in what you just said, these essential elements stand out: (1) The brightly lighted cavern whose walls seemed set with jewels, (2) The allusion to the Old Testament, and (3) The fact that the dream was related at Paserea Monastery. But knowing what we know and realizing all that happened, it's *absolutely impossible* that the dream wasn't known to Economu, who told it at once to Comrade Vogel with the advice that she call you and get you to tell it to her also, perhaps giving her an opportunity to find out further details."

"Yet I didn't tell it," whispered Farama.

"This remains to be verified. At any rate the content of the dream was accessible to Economu in the typed text of your statement, the text that he would have found on his desk anyway."

"I don't understand the connection," said Farama, looking first at one, then at the other.

"*Ei*, and it's this that seems hard to believe," the man with the yellowed teeth intervened brusquely, after offering Farama another cigarette. "Even *very hard to believe*, because then we'd have to imagine a series of coincidences so extraordinary that it would equal the mystery of the disappearance of Iozi and the other miracles in your tales."

"I don't very well understand your allusion . . ."

"If that's so, it means you're still very tired, because it's clear as daylight. Really, only the fact that Economu and Comrade Vogel were aware of the dream explains why Economu—who was one of the few people who knew that part of the Polish treasure was buried in Paserea Forest in the fall of 1939, and the only one who also knew that great quantities of gold and jewels still lay there undiscovered—only this explains, I say, why Economu decided to transport this treasure secretly one night to the cellar of his house on Calomfirescu Street, a house he'd requisitioned last spring. Something," the man added parenthetically, "that's impossible for you not to have found out at the time, because, as you repeated several times—it was confirmed by many witnesses in a concurrent investigation—you had the habit of walking *every day* through the entire Mantuleasa quarter, and whenever anyone happened to be moving you tried by various means to discover *who* it was."

Frightened, Farama listened with his hands lying forgotten in his lap, unable to tear his gaze away from the sad, weary smile of the speaker.

"And this is the only way to explain why a few weeks ago, under the pretext that water had started to rise in the cellar—a pretext he borrowed from your stories—Economu brought some workmen who were devoted to him and had them dig a hiding place in the depths of the cellar where he could deposit the gold and jewels from Paserea. We don't know precisely what his intentions were, but it's probable that, profiting by the position which he held, he would have sent the remnants of the treasure out of the country. Maybe he hoped, too, to interest Comrade Vogel in his plans and for that reason he suggested that she call you to tell her about Oana, and especially Oana's dream, with emphasis on that allusion to the blessedness of the Old Testament. I don't know to what extent Comrade Vogel allowed herself to be tempted by this plan; nevertheless it's surprising that she decides that the two of you will go riding together *after three o'clock* precisely on the night when Economu is to transport the treasure from Paserea Monastery to Calomfirescu Street, that is, two steps from Mantuleasa. And it's no less surprising that when he finds out by chance that he's been discovered, Economu kills himself in his office at 1:25, while only a few minutes later Comrade Vogel gets a phone call from some *strange source* and is informed that part of the Mantuleasa quarter will be closed off and searched by men on special duty, so she gives up the projected drive and at the same moment she doubts the veracity of your tales. It's hard to persuade ourselves that all these events are not related. On the contrary I think that up to now weariness has kept you from remember-

113

ing in minute detail the conversations that you had with Economu and Comrade Vogel. Your situation would be considerably improved if you would confirm for us by means of a clear, strong statement the connection between them, which you surely must have noticed as each one listened to you tell about Oana's wedding."

Farama looked into the man's eyes, frightened and pleading, as if he were imploring him to continue. "And all these things . . ." he murmured presently, "all these things happened just recently, a few hours ago?"

"No," said the man with the dark glasses. "You were, and still are, very tired. That's why you don't remember. These things took place three days ago, but because you were brought here in a condition of great weakness— total exhaustion—the doctor gave you a shot and since then you've been asleep."

"But don't worry," the other added, smiling. "All this time you've been fed artificially. If the regimen had been prolonged for a week you'd have gained at least two kilograms. . . ."

X

". . . YOU SEE," HE REALIZED THAT ONE OF THE MEN WAS saying, "things clear up. Some things explain other things. Together they form a structure, a configuration, and they unfold their meaning only if we accept this hypothesis: On the one hand you want to hide something, to keep a secret, while on the other your memory—like any memory—betrays you, that is, it fails to retain certain essential details and it keeps with precision, almost photographically, the peripheral episodes. It was enough, therefore, to examine with the necessary rigor these peripheral episodes in order to find the cipher by which the actions, characters, and ideas that you want to keep secret can be identified. This rigorous examination was made and I'll cite for you some of the conclusions at which we arrived.

"For reasons which remain to be explained, you try especially hard not to reveal the *real* relations between Darvari, Lixandru, and Marina, relations which, if we knew them, would have permitted us to understand the reason why Darvari decided to flee to Russia. I'll return presently to this complex, which I'll call Complex Number One. The second conclusion that was arrived at is this: Again for motives that remain to be determined you don't want to disclose the fact that, soon after Darvari's flight to Russia in 1931–32, Lixandru also decided to disappear, not like Iozi or Darvari, but in his own way, by changing his identity—that is, his name, occupation, and probably his appearance. Actually, after 1932 Lixandru no longer shows up in any of the places where he'd been known previously under this name—the Savings Bank, the Library of the Romanian Academy, the Chess Association, not to mention the restaurants and summer gardens he used to frequent and where no one remembers having seen him after 1932. On the other hand we have proof that he didn't die, nor did he leave the country permanently. We can't reject the possibility that he may have gone abroad in 1932 and returned later under another name. The fact is that nowhere within the territory of Romania, nor at any consulate abroad has there been a death registered under the name of Gheorghe P. Lixandru. Furthermore, according to your own statements it appears that you met him again by chance after 1932, but you don't say what he looked like or what you said, or how much time you were together—only a few minutes, several hours, or a whole day. We conclude that you haven't seen him for a long time, since you made such a desperate attempt this summer to ask Borza, whom you believed to be your former pupil, if he knew anything more about Lixandru; but of course this could have been only a feint. In other words, you're trying to find out if others know *what you know* about Lixandru. I repeat, this is only a hypothesis. . . ." He paused, and went on with a smile, "You don't seem very impressed with the reconstruction of Complex Number Two."

"I don't understand," whispered Farama. "Please believe me, it all seems like a dream. I remember very well,

I understand everything up to a point, and then there seems to be a blank and I no longer understand anything at all."

"You've been very tired," resumed the other, "but the special care that you're being given will soon take effect. Let's consider Complex Number One, to which an analysis of the different variations of Oana's wedding gives us a clue. I won't dwell upon the variations related to that prodigious performance of collective suggestion, illusionism, fakirism, or whatever, which the Doctor made at dawn; and I won't dwell either on the variations connected with the first meeting between the Doctor and the forester twenty years before, an adventure as fabulous as the incident of *boier* Calomfir, the disappearance of Iozi, or other incidents of this type. I don't dwell on these variations, because they're secondary and they lack importance for us; but let's come to the relationship of Darvari, Lixandru, and Marina. You said that the friendship between Lixandru and Darvari wasn't shaken that night, although many people thought the contrary." He opened the file and continued, "And yet in a previous statement you say that on that night Marina said to Darvari—I quote—'"Don't become an aviator! You'll never come back!" But Darvari looked at them both and replied, "I'm not afraid of death." "I wasn't talking about death," Marina added, "I tell you, *you won't come back*!" And then both youths burst out laughing. "Like Lixandru's arrow!" said Darvari, glancing at his friend; but Lixandru suddenly became serious again and tried to change the subject. "Today is Oana's wedding!" he exclaimed. "Today all that was fated has been fulfilled and it would be a pity to tempt God with other mysteries

117

and prophecies!" However, Darvari didn't let himself be persuaded so easily. "Maybe Marina knows something, too. Perhaps in her own way she knows the signs. Why not let her tell us what *'You'll never come back!'* means?"'

"But you see that discrepancies exist between what you said a few days ago and what you wrote on August 20—on the one hand, Lixandru, Darvari, and Marina were friendly enough when they talked together, and they talked about important things. On the other hand, the text written on August 20 reveals a growing tension between the two friends. It could be said, even, that Darvari tried to contradict every last thing Lixandru said, and to do exactly the contrary to what Lixandru wanted."

"Everything you've just mentioned," said Farama with some effort, "happened *before* Oana told them about the dream. It's true that later, when Darvari saw that Marina didn't leave Lixandru's side, he was sullen and quarrelsome, but I assure you they remained just as good friends as before."

"Of course, *apparently* they were just as good friends, but it's certain that deep inside something had changed. Surely Marina realized this because it's the only way to explain why, at dawn, when they were roused from the Doctor's enchantments, and after she'd spent all her time with Lixandru—I quote—'she took Darvari in her arms and cried so everyone could hear her, "If you love me as much as you say you do, will you wait for me ten years?" "I'll wait as long as you wish," Darvari replied. "I'll wait for you not ten, but twenty, fifty years!" "Then invite all these people to our wedding ten years from today, September 1930, right here at the Monastery, and Lixandru and Oana will be witnesses." "Not Lixandru," Darvari interrupted, "but the *Doftor* and Oana. . . ."' In your statement of August 20 from which I quoted you don't say what Lixandru's reaction was, but no doubt he was sad, because Marina quickly added, still addressing Darvari, '"But you must know that I'm too old for you. You think there's only a difference of five or six years, but I'm twenty years older than you are. I'm almost forty!" Everyone burst into laughter then, thinking that she was joking, but Darvari cried, "Even if you were fifty I'd still wait for you, because in 1930 you'd only be sixty and I know I'll love you far beyond old age!"'

"It's true, he said that," whispered Farama suddenly, as if he had just wakened.

"But it's obvious that this wedding which was to take place ten years later was a joke, something that Marina didn't believe would happen, that she couldn't believe. On the one hand she herself had warned Darvari not to become an aviator 'because he'd never come back.' On the other hand her cousin Dragomir was also there at the feast and everyone knew that they were supposed to have been engaged since childhood, because that's what the family had decided, so the 'line wouldn't die out.' Only one conclusion is implied—Marina did all this to pacify Darvari. Hence, she'd sensed the break between Darvari and Lixandru."

"And yet," observed Farama, "I remember a comment of Comrade Minister Vogel . . ."

"Comrade Vogel's no longer Minister. She's been given another assignment. . . . Now let's return to Complex Number One. Although it was a joke, Darvari took Marina's promise seriously, but from here on things are no longer clear and we wonder why. Deficient memory?

Lack of interest in all that happened from 1920 to the disappearance of Darvari ten years later in the summer of 1930? Or was it simply your decision to *conceal* at any price certain events which, if known, would have revealed to us not only the motives for Darvari's flight, but that would also have indicated the meaning of Lixandru's metamorphosis? Personally, I'm inclined toward this latter hypothesis and I'll try to show you why. Actually, what have you told us, in so many interrogations and in so many hundreds of written pages, about the ties between Darvari, Lixandru, and Marina from 1920 to 1930? Pretty much the same things—very few—that you've restated and told over again countless times. I'll summarize them. You say that several times Marina confessed to Darvari that she was really twenty—or even thirty—years older than he. I quote: '"That's why Dragomir doesn't dare marry me," she told him. "He knows my age."'

"Once, in 1925–26, she showed him her birth certificate—and you specify that the document had been issued abroad—and this would have made her almost sixty at that time. Darvari looked at her in fright, and you add, 'not because he had found out her age but because when he looked at her he saw suddenly that she was truly old. "If you still love me now that you've learned that I'll soon be sixty, I give you permission to kiss me!"' 'Darvari,' you write, 'was dumbfounded and turned pale, his glance fixed upon her, and then Marina exclaimed suddenly with great exultation in her voice, "You see, such is the love of men—tied to the body. The spirit, for you, glows only around youthful forms!"' The next moment she flees from the salon into the adjoining room

120

and returns after a few minutes looking just as young as she had seemed on the night when Darvari saw her the first time in the tavern of Fanica Tunsu in 1919. Darvari falls to his knees, but she no longer permits him to kiss her. '"However, I forgive you this time too," she told him, smiling. "Because being naive like all men you think I made myself up as an old woman and after frightening you I pitied you and washed my face, but I tell you again that I'm really old, as my birth certificate proves. . . ." Darvari smiled happily as he listened to her because at that time the woman before him seemed to be around twenty or twenty-five!'

"Your statement isn't clear about what happened after that. You say only that Marina liked the theater, imitating her ancestress Arghira on this point also. You say she was accustomed to dress curiously, eccentrically, and that sometimes she seemed really old because she powdered her hair or made herself up in the manner of old women when they want to look young. Do you think, therefore, that when she showed him her birth certificate she had made up her face to look really sixty?"

"I thought that for a long time," Farama said very softly, "but I was mistaken."

"You probably were mistaken, because from your own account it would seem that on that day Darvari didn't see *at first* how old she was. He only saw this *after* she showed him the birth certificate. It was, then, a question of something else, a special technique that Marina had of altering her appearance at will.

"And now we come to the final—and the most important—episode, which unfortunately you have always related very succinctly. It's the matter of that night in the summer of 1930, when for unknown reasons Marina detains Darvari to sleep with her and they go to bed together for the first time. I say for unknown reasons because we may wonder why she hadn't done it before, why she waited ten years to go to bed with Darvari, and why she did so only a few weeks before the wedding. Anyway, from your successive narrations, we gather that on that evening the two young people entertained themselves until a late hour in a garden near Cotroceni, and Darvari seemed more in love than ever. On that evening Marina was dressed as she had never been before—with extraordinary elegance, though discreetly—and she looked younger perhaps than when Dararvi had met her eleven years earlier. Her face was like that of a child, without a bit of powder or a trace of paint.

"I've summarized your text of August 20 and I don't quite understand what happened later. The young couple spent the night together. Toward morning Darvari woke up and leaned over his beloved to kiss her, but in the uncertain light of dawn, you write, 'he saw with horror that Marina was an old woman, much older than he'd discovered her to be a few years before after seeing her birth certificate.' You write that he stared at her, stunned, for a long time and then rose from the bed, careful not to wake her, and began to get dressed. When he had almost finished he realized that Marina was smiling and watching him. '"I know what you're going to do," Marina must have said, "but don't be commonplace like everyone else. Attempt the great flight! Climb, climb, climb, and never stop!" And then she cried in a voice that was strangely jubilant, "I'll give you a talisman and at a certain moment you'll meet Lixandru's arrow!"' But it isn't certain that

Darvari heard the last words. He'd left in silence, carefully closing the door behind him.

"All these things, you say, you found out later from Lixandru, who had learned them from Marina that very day, because if I understand correctly, Marina dressed too, on the spot, and left to look for Lixandru; but she didn't find him until later in the day, at noon. After she told him everything that had happened, she added, '"Try to stop him, because I suspect he intends to run away by plane and he's in great danger because he doesn't know what he's doing." "Is he in danger because you didn't get to give him the talisman?" inquired Lixandru.' (It's hard to guess if he were serious or joking). '"No, this was only a metaphor, and he didn't understand it," Marina would have replied. "I haven't any talisman and everything I told him about the 'great flight' was only to test him, to teach him not to let himself be bewitched by appearances again, because last night I wasn't twenty years old as he thought, and this morning I wasn't over sixty, as I seemed to be. I'm the age that I am. . . ."' (And you add that Lixandru, regarding her, still thought she was between twenty-five and thirty.) Anyway, Lixandru reached the airport too late and managed to talk to the chief of the squadron only after waiting for several hours. In the meantime Darvari had landed at Constanta, refueled, and flown on toward the east. . . ."

"If that's how it happened," the man resumed after a pause, "It would have been more beautiful than a folk tale and sadder than the saddest love story. . . . But, you see, you declared that you learned all this from Lixandru and only from him. You didn't meet Marina again after 1925–26. (In one draft you say you met Darvari around that same time and that he told you something about—I quote—'the enchantments and charms of Marina,' assuring you however that he was still in love, and reminding you that you were invited to the wedding in September 1930.) But there are a lot of details that contradict the Lixandru version. In the first place it was impossible even in 1930 for a pilot to go to the airport, climb into a plane and take off without precise orders and instructions. If he did it, it means that he had planned the flight in advance and especially that he had accomplices in Bucuresti and Constanta. And even if no doubt exists that it is a question of premeditation (since this was what the investigation revealed), no complicity could ever have been proven. *For us* this carries a special significance. Several hypotheses can be proposed, the first and most plausible being as follows: Darvari plans the flight down to the last detail, with accomplices whom we don't know, but we suspect where we have to look for them. We can't know with precision what Darvari's mission was, but considering the date of the flight—*August* 1930—we know at least the *meaning* of this mission. Although their friendship was no longer what it had been, Darvari disclosed to Lixandru at the last moment the decision he'd made. At present we don't know what Lixandru's role was in the disappearance of Darvari, and we can't know it until we resolve Complex Number Two, that is, until we learn the *new identity* assumed by Lixandru after 1932; because only by knowing *who he became* after 1932 will we know the role he played in the flight and disappearance of Dararvi. And then we'll also know something else—if he's *with* us or *against* us."

"And now I'll ask you a question—a single

question—which you'll probably refuse to answer immediately, but we'll find it out anyway eventually. You've known for a long time the new identity of Lixandru, but you know something else too. You know that this new identity has concealed him so well that Lixandru has become completely unrecognizable to all those who weren't witnesses to both identities, and especially to those who weren't present at the metamorphosis, I'd call it, of the youth he was until that time in 1931–32 into the man he became after this date. It happens that you are the *only* witness to this metamorphosis, and that's why you're of inestimable value to us. If Lixandru became unrecognizable for all the others *he can be anyone* in this country. He can be one of us. He can even be one of our most outstanding men, one of those who determine the destinies of our nation today. *Ei bine*, my question then is this: *Who* is Lixandru, *here and now*, in this city, perhaps even in this building? You know him. Tell us. Who is he?"

XI

THAT YEAR SUMMER CAME UNEXPECTEDLY EARLY. WHEN
Farama started out for a stroll in the early afternoon he
stayed close to the fences in the shade of the trees, glancing into the gardens, stopping at times before trees that
were weighed down with apricots and cherries, as if he
expected to see children go scrambling up them. He
would rouse himself after a while and then hasten his
step, going toward one of the benches on which he liked
to rest. If he found the bench already occupied he would
lift his hat politely and ask permission to sit down. After
a few moments he would ask the time and just as politely
express his thanks, but he would not encourage conver-
sation. If the other continued to talk he would listen for a
while, nodding his head slowly, then he would get up,
lift his hat, and proceed on his way.

One hot afternoon early in July he saw the empty
bench from afar and he was glad, because he felt tired.
He sat down with effort, took out his handkerchief and
wrapped it around his neck, fanning himself with his
hat. The street was deserted. Soon drowsiness was upon
him and he placed his hat beside him on the bench,
leaned his head on the palm of his right hand, and closed
his eyes. Awaking with a start a few moments later, he
found seated near him on the bench a man whose face he
could not see because his back was turned.

"Please forgive me," said the old man. "I suppose I was dozing. It's very warm," he added as he began again to fan himself.

The stranger turned his head and smiled at him, but at once he resumed reading the magazine that he held in his hand. Presently a boy passed in front of them, his mouth and hands blackened with mulberry juice. Smiling, Farama followed him with his eyes.

"I'm sorry to bother you," he said, after a moment, "but can you tell me the time?"

"Two—five past," replied the other without turning around.

"Thank you very much. I have an appointment at a quarter after, half-past. I can rest here a moment longer. It's very warm. . . ."

The stranger turned to him and smiled again, nodding his head. He went back to his reading, but a moment later he paused abruptly and looked at Farama, puzzled. Then he reopened his magazine.

"You've changed a lot since I last saw you, *domnule* Principal," he murmured without raising his eyes from the review. "Probably you too have had a lot of trouble. I hardly recognized you. . . ."

Farama was silent, continuing to fan himself with his hat.

"You don't remember me now. I was a pupil at Mantuleasa School many—very many—years ago. You have nothing now to remind you of me. I'm Borza, Borza I. Vasile."

"Borza? Borza I. Vasile?" repeated Farama, laying his hat on his knees. "How curious!" he added, sighing.

"Do you remember how I broke my head once falling

127

from an apricot tree and you took me in your arms and carried me into the teacher's room in order to dress my injury? And the next day was the celebration of the Tenth of May?"

"Yes, yes," said Farama, "I seem to remember; but I wonder can it be true?" He stood up with some difficulty and bowed several times. "Unfortunately I have to leave because I have an appointment at two-fifteen, two-thirty. And it's become terribly warm. . . . I'm glad to have met you," he added.

The stranger laid his magazine beside him on the bench and lit a cigarette thoughtfully. After Farama had disappeared around the corner of the street, someone came out of a nearby courtyard and walked toward the bench.

"Did you find out anything?" he asked without sitting down.

"No. He pretended not to recognize me. It wasn't hard," he added, standing up and trying to stuff the magazine into the pocket of his jacket. "I repeated the few sentences I'd memorized, and I don't suppose I was convincing. Or perhaps he found out in the meantime that Borza is no longer alive, and that made me suspect from the start."

They walked side by side.

"And yet," the other man said presently, very softly, "I must regain his trust. He was at Anca's the night it all happened, and then he was questioned by Number One and Number Three. He knows a lot of things and he's the *only one* who knows them. We'll have to try again. . . ."

They stopped at the corner of the street and the first man murmured, "You try, Lixandru."

ABOUT THE AUTHOR

Mircea Eliade (1907–1986) was born in Bucharest, Romania; he received his doctorate from the University of Bucharest in 1932, after several years of study at the University of Calcutta. Eliade's first publications were in fiction, and he continued to write plays and stories as well as scholarly works over the course of sixty years. He became a professor at the Ecole des Hautes Etudes, Sorbonne, and lectured at the universities of Rome, Lund, Marburg, Munich, Frankfurt, Padua, and Strasbourg. He helped to establish the history of religions as a field in the United States when he arrived in 1956, joining the faculty of the University of Chicago. At the time of his death, Eliade was Professor in the Divinity School and the Committee on Social Thought at the University of Chicago.

Eliade's many publications available in English include: *The Forge and the Crucible: The Origins and Structures of Alchemy; Occultism, Witchcraft, and Cultural Fashions; Zalmoxis, the Vanishing God: Comparative Studies in the Religions and Folklore of Dacia and Eastern Europe; The Quest: History and Meaning in Religion; The Two and the One; Ordeal by Labyrinth: Conversations with Claude-Henri Rocquet; A History of Religious Ideas* (in three volumes); and his *Autobiography* (in two volumes).